The Warning

by

Jonas Saul

PUBLISHED BY:

Imagine Press Inc.
Ebook ISBN: 978-0-9869376-6-8
Paperback ISBN: 978-1-998047-02-4
Hardcover ISBN: 978-1-998047-18-5

The Warning
Copyright © 2011 by Jonas Saul

The Sarah Roberts Series

Dark Visions (One)
The Warning (Two)
The Crypt (Three)
The Hostage (Four)
The Victim (Five)
The Enigma (Six)
The Vigilante (Seven)
The Rogue (Eight)
Killing Sarah (Nine)
The Antagonist (Ten)
The Redeemed (Eleven)
The Haunted (Twelve)
The Unlucky (Thirteen)
The Abandoned (Fourteen)
The Cartel (Fifteen)
Losing Sarah (Sixteen)
The Pact (Seventeen)
The Terror (Eighteen)
The Chase (Nineteen)
The Betrayal (Twenty)
Sarah's Return (Twenty-One)
The Hunt (Twenty-Two)
The Delivery (Twenty-Three)
The Trap (Twenty-Four)
The Ultimatum (Twenty-Five)
The Depraved (Twenty-Six)
The Condemned (Twenty-Seven)
Payback (Twenty-Eight)
The Unknown (Twenty-Nine)
Wrath (Thirty)
The Damned (Thirty-One)
The Game (Thirty-Two)

The Decoy (Thirty-Three)
The Disappearance (Thirty-Four)
The Whole Truth (Thirty-Five)
Alex (Thirty-Six)
Parkman (Thirty-Seven)
Darwin (Thirty-Eight)
Aaron (Thirty-Nine)
Remains To Be Seen (Forty)

The Jake Wood Novels

The Immortal Gene (Book One)
The Immortal Target (Book Two)

Standalone Novels

'Til Death Do Us Part
The Drowning
The Woman in the Woods
The Threat
The Specter
The Mafia Trilogy
A Murder in Time
Frequency of the Dead

Co-Authored Novels

Collision Course (Written with Gary Ponzo)
There Will Be Blood (Written with Rania Stone)
The Soulless (Written with Rania Stone)

Short Story Collections

Twisted Fate (Tales of Horror)

Twists of Fate (Tales of Hope)

Chapter 1

THE WOODS WERE DARKER and more ominous this time.

Jack Tate tightened his grip on the terrier's leash, drawing the small dog closer to him. A soft breeze wafted past his face. The darkening sky revealed a purple hue, offering little comfort.

Something about the woods bothered him. He slowed, watching the trees ahead.

He wondered why he was making such a big deal about it. He had done this walk hundreds of times. This wasn't a high-crime area.

What could go wrong?

A soft hum emanated from the woods—the trees billowing in the breeze.

The leash loosened as Champ moved closer to Jack's leg.

"Hello?" he called out to the line of trees. "Anybody there?" It was foolish calling into the trees as if he were a child afraid of the bogeyman.

Champ tugged on the leash, pulling toward the trees.

Jack knelt to touch the top of the dog's head and offered calming words. He scanned the area again and saw no one around. Champ tugged on the leash harder.

Jack walked toward the trees, his small dog in tow. A minute later, he entered the woods.

"Hello?" he called out again.

Foolish, he chastised himself.

Champ's tugging became bothersome, but it made him realize why the dog was insistent. He always let Champ off the leash to run free when they entered the woods on their evening walks.

He unclipped the leash from Champ's collar. The terrier bolted away, down the path and around a corner. He was gone from sight in seconds. Jack called after him, but it was no use.

His nerves were firing. Hairs were rising, stomach moving around. Remaining aware of his surroundings, Jack started after his dog.

The deeper he moved into the woods, the darker it got. He caught a glimpse of the sky between the branches above. Dark purple clouds sat motionlessly. There were less than twenty minutes of light left in the day. Even though it was cool out, he perspired under his shirt.

He caressed the rip at the base of his shirt. The two-inch cut had been made with scissors, sliced on an angle near the bottom button. He twirled the edges of the cut through his fingers, seeking comfort that remained elusive.

Trees surrounded him. He called out to the terrier again but received no response. Past the halfway mark on the walking path, he concluded that continuing forward would be a quicker route home as the trail led back to the corner of his street.

He spun at the sight of movement to his left. He stopped walking and stared. Champ was digging in the dirt twenty feet away.

"Champ, come here, boy."

The dog ignored him and continued to dig with his front paws. Champ was clearly on a mission, as if he were uncovering an old bone buried for later consumption.

With the sunlight dimming fast, Jack stepped into the foliage after his dog. Champ didn't look up once. He kept digging as Jack drew closer.

Jack stumbled through the thick foliage and almost fell twice. He attached the leash clip back onto the dog's collar with just enough light left for him to see what he was doing. Under cover of the trees, it was darker than in the open.

The terrier continued his resistance with the leash.

"Come on, Champ. Stop pulling on the leash so much."

Champ's behavior was so unlike him. He wasn't usually like this. Jack bent to pick the dog up, but something caused him to stop short.

Champ had partially uncovered something. Jack stumbled to the nearest tree, one hand holding himself up, the other holding his stomach. This time when Champ pulled on the leash, Jack tugged it back in anger.

"Stop it. That is enough."

Jack collected his dog and stumbled out of the woods, mentally marking the spot where Champ had made his discovery.

Fifteen minutes later, he was on the phone reporting the dead body to the police.

Chapter 2

JACK TATE SAT ON the sawed-off trunk of a dead tree. A cop who identified himself as Winnfield stood over him, flipping notebook pages back and forth.

"Let me get this straight." The cop raised his pen in the air. "You are out for a walk. You go into the woods and let your dog run loose off the leash. Your dog runs away from you, but then you locate him. When you pick the terrier up, you see part of a decomposed face. Is that about it? That's your statement?"

Jack nodded and looked down at his shoes. The lights on the three cruisers rotated ten feet away, flashing in his eyes.

"Something doesn't fit."

Jack looked back up at the cop. It was late, and he was tired of talking. He'd committed no crime, nor was he going to defend himself.

Champ lay asleep at his feet. He only wished his stomach was as calm as his dog. It was all happening again. He was being summoned, and he knew it.

The cop said, "After last night and this morning's rain, the ground holding the body is soft. That's probably why, fifteen feet off the beaten path, your dog would be drawn over by the smell." Officer Winnfield paused and flipped another page in his notebook. "We found your footprint impressions in the dirt beside your dog's paw prints. But we found no other recent impressions in the soil."

Jack tried to rise from the tree stump, but Officer Winnfield touched Jack's shoulder to ease him back down. Jack almost asked out loud, *what the hell was that for?* Instead, he chose to keep quiet.

"So, explain it to me again."

He groaned in frustration. Next time he wouldn't call the cops. He'd let some kids playing in the woods find the dead body.

"I was walking my dog. He got away from me. When I found him, he'd dug up a surprise. Write it up that way. Now, I need to get home. Are we done here?"

Officer Winnfield folded the notebook and slid it into a breast pocket in his uniform.

"You sound angry, Mr. Tate. Please understand I'm only doing my job. I have one more question."

Jack rolled his hand in the air in a gesture for the cop to go ahead and ask his question.

"Why is your shirt torn at the base?"

Jack looked down at his fingers as they rolled around the rip. Since the incident almost twenty years ago, he would only wear shirts with this exact tear. For the most part, it wasn't noticeable as he tucked his shirts in. The reason for the cut was something he could never tell a cop, partly because he wasn't *supposed* to remember what really happened. If he told a cop the truth, he would be arrested.

"I cut it accidentally with scissors when removing the tags." As soon as he said it, Jack felt his voice lacked confidence. "What has that got to do with anything?"

"Stay right here," Officer Winnfield said. "Don't move until I come back."

The cop walked over to a man in a suit. The suit looked like he was in charge. People dressed all in white set up lights and various apparatus around the makeshift grave. Other people were bent over, sifting dirt away to get to the rest of the body.

Jack stroked Champ's head. "This will all be over soon," he said. The terrier lifted his head a notch and then dropped it again, completely oblivious to the serious commotion going on around him.

Officer Winnfield walked back over and stood in front of Jack. "You're going to have to come with us."

Jack stood up. "Why's that?"

"Is there someone you could give your dog to?"

"Am I under arrest or something? What did I do?"

"Mr. Tate, please listen to me. Is there someone who can take your terrier?"

Jack sat back down on the stump. *What's going on? How serious is this?*

Spectators had gathered around the yellow tape the police had used to seal off the area.

"Glenda over there," Jack said and pointed. "She takes Champ when I'm away for any length of time. You can give my dog to her. She's the one in the white housecoat."

Winnfield took the leash and walked away with Champ.

Jack remained sitting, his knee bobbing. He had nothing

to do with this. Why would they think otherwise?

The temperature had dropped further, leaving the evening with a subtle chill. Jack shivered under the assault of his own sweat.

Moments later, Officer Winnfield stood in front of him again.

"Jack Tate, please stand up."

"What's going on here?" Jack asked.

"We're going to continue our questioning at the police station."

"Am I under arrest?"

"Not at this time."

"So, I find this person buried in the ground while walking my dog, call you guys about it, and you make me feel guilty? Does that about sum it up?"

"We're just trying to figure everything out," Officer Winnfield said as he put a hand on Jack's arm and guided him to a cruiser.

"Why all the suspicion? Why are you taking me in for questioning?"

"It's that rip on the bottom of your shirt," Winnfield said.

Jack frowned. "The rip?"

"There's an identical rip, in the exact same spot, on the shirt the dead girl is wearing."

Chapter 3

Two hours passed before an officer opened the interrogation room door and offered Jack a bathroom break.

Minutes later, he retook his seat behind a drab metal table on a hard steel chair. The room was a classic crime movie setup, complete with a wall of glass and a solitary light hanging from the ceiling.

"Feeling better?" Officer Winnfield asked.

Winnfield looked refreshed, as if he had taken a nap followed by an injection of caffeine. Jack chose not to answer the stupid question.

Winnfield adjusted his shirt in front of the two-way mirror and turned back to Jack.

"What can you tell me about the girl?" Winnfield asked.

Jack glared at the cop. "She's dead." His patience had thinned. This was getting ridiculous.

Winnfield pulled back as if surprised. Jack put it all together in that second. *He's new at this.*

The two-hour wait was meant to rattle Jack. Winnfield's

swagger when he stepped into the room and the posturing in front of the mirror showed that *I got this* confidence.

"Okay, is that how you want to play it?" Winnfield asked.

"I'm not playing. I already told you everything I knew at the crime scene. You've wasted both our time bringing me here."

Winnfield leaned forward and dropped his hands on the table with a solid thump. "Start by telling me about the rip in the shirt. Why does the girl have the same one?"

Jack looked down at his lap. He had been anticipating this question. He looked back up, met Winnfield's eyes, and said nothing.

Winnfield tried again. "Why does the girl's shirt have the same rip?"

The officer stood to his full height and paced in front of the two-way mirror.

"Here's what I see happening," Jack said. "You've held me for over two hours, and for what, to ask me the same question you already asked me back in the woods? Release me or charge me with something because I have no idea why the girl's shirt is ripped."

Winnfield stopped pacing and leaned against the mirror.

"You're in a lot of trouble, Mr. Tate."

A buzzer sounded twice. Winnfield opened the door and stepped out. Minutes later, the door opened again, and two men entered.

"You're free to go, Mr. Tate, but stay local. We may want to be in touch." One of the men held the door open for him.

"Someone gonna give me a ride back?" Jack asked.

"You're free to go, Mr. Tate. You're on your own."

Both men escorted Jack to the main door of the building and then walked away, leaving him there.

With nothing left to do, Jack paid for a cab and got home after midnight. When the taxi pulled away, he looked at Glenda's house and debated if it was too late to get Champ. He decided to leave him for the night.

The air was calm and cool. Jack breathed in and sighed. He had a lot of work ahead of him.

The ripped shirt meant *they* had made a mistake. The fact that the body was found so close to his house was another message. It was so long ago. He couldn't remember the exact details. The bullet had erased part of his memory. He knew that he was lucky to be alive.

On the walkway to his house, a light flickered past an upstairs window. He stopped and stared, but the windows stayed dark now.

He eased up to the porch quietly and waited. With his breathing under control, he reached for his keys. He had done this sort of thing years ago when he was a cop. He didn't need memory to use instinct.

A creaking noise sounded from just inside the house. He froze. Someone was on the other side of the door.

He stepped away from the door.

Cold steel pressed against his neck.

"Don't be stupid," a man said from behind him. "And don't make any noise."

Jack lifted his hands slowly, his house keys falling to the porch. His stomach dropped with them.

"Move away from the door and keep your hands where I can see them, but don't raise them too high. It looks dumb and may alert a neighbor."

Jack stepped off the porch and onto the lawn. The man behind him stayed close. The front door opened and closed.

"Did you find anything?"

"No," a new voice said.

"Okay, let's move. Jack, do you see the red van on the other side of the street? That's where we're going. Has anyone seen any sign of that fucking girl yet?"

The other guy didn't answer him.

The street was empty. Directly across the road, movement caught Jack's eye.

Speak of the devil.

A tall girl with blonde hair flowing past her shoulders from under a red bandanna stepped out from behind a tree.

She lifted her arms in a sleek, precise movement, the gun in her hand reflecting the streetlight.

Then her gun spit out a silenced bullet. The cold steel pressed against Jack's neck moved away. The man holding the weapon grunted as he hit the ground. He grasped his leg around the knee, where blood gushed past his fingers.

The girl moved fast. She was already standing beside the second man, gun tip aimed low, telling him to give her his weapons or he would lose a knee, too.

Jack stepped aside and leaned against the van, amazed at the girl's methodical efficiency.

She stowed the man's gun in a shoulder holster, kneed him in the groin, and pistol-whipped him unconscious in one fluid motion.

Then she turned to address Jack. "My name is Sarah Roberts. You're safe for now, but you're coming with me."

Chapter 4

SARAH PULLED THE CAR around a corner, drove to the back of a strip mall, and parked behind a dumpster. All that time, she kept a close eye on her new passenger.

Once she had parked the car, she brought her gun around to aim it at him.

"What's your name?" she asked, holding the gun firm. Her eyes moved to the mirrors to ensure they weren't being watched.

The man appeared frightened and intimidated, but she couldn't be sure if it were a show. He leaned his head against the passenger window, gazing absently out the front.

"Your name?" Sarah asked again.

"Jack Tate." He looked sideways at her. "What is this?"

Sarah pushed the gun forward. "I said, you don't ask questions." Her teeth clenched when she spoke. "I do not enjoy repeating myself."

He shrugged. "Okay, okay."

"Who were those men?" she asked. "What did they

want?"

Jack motioned with his hands to his mouth, asking if he could talk.

"Test me, come on, test me. We'll see who leaves this car in one piece. I said, *no questions*. I didn't say you couldn't talk. So, talk. Tell me who those men were."

"I don't know who they were."

"I hate having to shoot people I don't know or who haven't threatened me, but I had no choice."

Jack nodded and continued to look out the windshield.

"That van in the street they were taking you to wasn't their vehicle."

Jack turned to her.

"They broke the lock on the back door. Their car was a few houses down. I watched the whole thing."

Jack motioned with his hands to talk.

"Do that again, and each hand wins a prize, courtesy of my friend, Smith & Wesson." Sarah moved the gun to aim at Jack's hands.

"I need to ask a question," he said.

Sarah nodded. "Okay, go."

"Why were they taking me to the van?"

"Who knows? Probably to kill you."

Jack looked away. "If that was the case and you know so much about what they were doing, why don't you know who they are? For that matter, why don't you know me? You stepped in and saved me." He paused for a second and then added. "I'd like to know how you came by all this information. Are you in on it somehow?"

"I was told to be there."

She saw the same reaction a hundred times.

Bewilderment and disbelief, coupled with a look of, *what a strange thing to say.*

"Who told you?" he asked. "And why?"

"It seems we've passed the no-questions phase rather quickly. Fine, I'll give you the short answer because it's too long a story. I'm looking for a murderer who got away about twenty years ago, and somehow you're connected to him. You're either him, or you know him. The message wasn't completely accurate."

Jack leaned his head back and shut his eyes.

"Your response tells me you know something about what I just said," Sarah added.

He opened his eyes and sat up straighter. "I do not know what you're talking about."

"Whether you tell me or not, I'll find out."

Jack fidgeted with his hands on his lap. "It's not that I don't want to tell you. It's that I can't."

"Why?"

"I was shot twenty years ago. If you're after someone who committed crimes in that era, and you have somehow discovered that I was connected to that person, you're about to be sadly disappointed."

"Why?"

"I discovered who a serial killer was. He terrorized and killed young girls throughout the Midwest back then. I was shot in the head and left for dead. It took years to regain enough memory to live independently and function." He glanced at her. "I was a cop. I live on my pension now. I still have horrible, recurring nightmares." He shook his head and looked away from Sarah. "I have scars from the bullet wound and my assailant's knife."

"He stabbed you, too?"

"In the midsection, here," Jack said and pointed down below his belly button where the shirt was ripped. "After I got shot in the head, I was coherent for a few minutes. I was losing strength. The knife had cut a two-inch slit at the base of my shirt when he stabbed me. I couldn't lift the shirt over my bleeding head, but I could rip it off because of the knife slit. I wrapped it around my head to staunch the blood flow before I passed out. It took almost three hours for them to find me. I would've died if my shirt wasn't stuck to the wound on my head. That's why there's a rip here." He motioned to the bottom of his shirt. "It's in honor of that time. It's a reminder for me of a life-changing experience."

"You seem to remember a lot for a guy who claims to have had amnesia," Sarah said as she scanned the parking lot for movement again. "Then why was the shirt ripped on the girl found in the woods by your house?"

"I have no idea," Jack said. "Wait a second, how do you know about that?"

Ignoring his question, Sarah pressed on. "Why would two goons be sent to execute you?"

"Nothing makes sense," Jack said as if in a daze.

Sarah set the safety on her gun and placed it on her lap between her thighs. She dropped the car into drive and started moving again.

"What are we going to do?" Jack asked.

"I don't know yet. I'll ask my sister. She'll know."

"Who's your sister? Where is she?"

"My sister's name is Vivian, and she's dead."

Chapter 5

BLAKE ROLLED ON THE ground and then lightly touched his wounded crotch.

Who the hell was that girl?

She had knocked him out cold. He touched the side of his head where blood had crusted up in a scab. There would be hell to pay for this.

At least I'm not the one who got shot.

He walked over to Marco and touched his neck. A slow and steady pulse. Blood spread out from Marco's unconscious body on the concrete. It was not enough to kill him, but he would need medical treatment soon.

Blake grabbed under Marco's armpits and dragged him toward Jack Tate's house. He was inside the front foyer within a minute, winded and out of breath. After setting Marco down, he got a paring knife from the kitchen and trotted back to Marco.

Blake jabbed the knife in and out of Marco's inner thigh without pausing, looking to sever the femoral artery.

Marco's body jumped and jerked as the blood flowed from the new wound without waking him.

Blake tossed the knife away, plugged Marco's nose, and covered his mouth. Marco was gone a moment later without more than a whimper.

He washed his hands in Jack's guest bathroom and stepped back into the foyer. He looked down at his friend. They had done a lot of jobs in the last year together.

Too bad a girl got the jump on you, old friend.

He pulled out his cell phone and dialed.

"We missed the mark," Blake said when the phone was answered.

"How is that? Explain it to me."

"Marco fucked up. The girl came out of nowhere. We were moving toward the van on the street. We kept an eye out for her. She shot Marco, pistol whipped me, and took Tate."

"This doesn't make sense. How can a girl take out both of you?"

"Marco's fault again. He had his gun jammed in Tate's neck. Mine was holstered. Look, it won't happen again. I dragged Marco off the street into Tate's foyer." Blake walked across the hall into the living room. He parted the drapes and looked out at the street. It amazed him that no one heard anything. It must've been at least fifteen minutes since the girl showed up, which meant it was time to move.

"What's Marco doing now?"

"Nothing. He's dead. I used Tate's kitchen knife to open an artery in his leg."

Blake listened to the breathing on the other end of the phone.

"Good. Someone had to pay for this. I want the girl dead.

You got anything on her? Anything to help identify her or where she might go?"

"Nothing. It happened too fast. She had long blond hair and a red bandanna."

"A red bandanna?"

Blake stepped away from the curtains and started for the house's back door. "Yeah, a bandanna. Why is that important?"

"That confirms who she is. You just met Sarah Roberts."

Chapter 6

SARAH HAD DECIDED TO stay off the road and hide in a motel. She paid cash at the front desk and parked outside the motel room door, backing her Kia up for an easy exit if needed.

Once in the room, she handcuffed Jack to the bathroom sink so he could sleep in the bathtub with one arm dangling out. After much protest, she made him comfortable with blankets and a pillow, shut the bathroom door, and lay on the bed to think. She had to try to understand the messages. That was always the hard part.

The TV's remote control sat on the night table beside her. She hit the power button and lowered the volume just enough to drown out Jack's occasional plea from the bathroom. The motel's courtesy paper and pen were her companions in bed as she searched the news channels for anything on the guy she had shot earlier.

A half-hour later, Jack had fallen quiet, and nothing was on the news.

Sarah wondered why Jack Tate was important. She

thought she was supposed to meet her sister's murderer tonight. Or would Jack lead her to the murderer she sought? She had no way of knowing. The message wasn't that specific. It just said the street name, the house number, and the man she was to meet. It also stated *Vivian*, which meant that this person was connected to her dead sister somehow.

As the adrenaline wore off, sleepiness settled over her.

Then the familiar numbness of a blackout came over her hand. She welcomed it by grabbing the pen, resting on the bed, and closing her eyes.

Seconds later, she sat up and looked at the pad.

Tate knows more than he's saying.

Sarah jumped from the bed, picked up her gun, checked that the safety was off, and barged into the bathroom. Jack lay curled up in the tub in an awkward position, sleeping.

"What happened to you tonight?" Sarah shouted.

He jerked in surprise, opened his eyes, and lifted his head. "What?"

"What happened to you? Why were those men trying to kill you?" Sarah asked. She shut the toilet lid and sat, keeping the gun hidden behind her thigh.

"I have no idea," Jack said, shutting his eyes again and resting his head.

"You've got to do better than that."

"I mean it. I have no idea." Jack explained what happened earlier in the evening, starting with him walking his dog, Champ, the body he found, the police response, and finishing with the two guys waiting at his house.

"Why would the police respond the way they did if you were just walking your dog and happened upon a body?"

"I have no idea," he repeated.

"Can you identify the girl you saw tonight?" She lifted the gun, so it sat across her thighs. He was lying. His eyes gave him away.

"Who are you?" Jack asked. "Where did you come from?" He turned to see her better. "I should be asking you a few serious questions. You're the one who will be brought up on kidnapping charges when this is all over."

"You're wasting my time. I need to know if you recognized the girl you found buried in the woods."

Jack shook his head. "No, I did not recognize her."

Sarah got up and stepped from the bathroom. She had heard her name on the TV. A news anchor was talking about the shooting and stabbing death in the home of Jack Tate. Police were now looking for Jack and a girl known as Sarah Roberts.

"*It's unclear how Sarah Roberts is involved,*" the anchor said. "*An anonymous tip said that Sarah Roberts shot the man found dead at the scene.*"

Sarah ran back into the bathroom, undid the handcuffs, and ushered Jack out.

"What now?" he asked.

"We have to move. The police will be here soon. Nowhere is safe because someone knows I have you, and they know me."

"Where are we going?" Jack asked.

Sarah gripped the doorknob, her gun held high in the other hand.

"To get answers."

Chapter 7

SARAH GRABBED HER CELL phone and dialed a familiar number two miles from the motel. It was after three in the morning. She didn't expect an answer, but it was picked up on the second ring.

"Dolan here."

"That was fast," Sarah said. "You must've been awake."

"You know, I felt I should stay up late tonight."

"Do you realize how corny that sounds coming from a renowned psychic? Listen, Dolan, I need your help."

"What's going on?"

"I'll tell you when I see you. Can we meet somewhere?"

"Sure, come to my house."

Sarah hung up and dropped her cell phone in the console. Up ahead, she saw a deserted strip mall. She turned right, bounced over a speed bump, and guided the car around to the back alley behind two dumpsters. She parked and turned to face Jack. He'd been quiet since they left the motel. She guessed it was fatigue with all he'd been through in the last twelve hours.

Sarah had to assume that Jack Tate wasn't her sister's murderer. He claimed to be an ex-cop. Vivian would have tried harder to warn her who she was traveling with if he was. He was important in some way, though. Important enough to keep around, at least until she figured everything out.

She smacked his arm to get his attention. "We have to get a few things clear."

Jack nodded. "Okay, I'm listening."

"I'm hunting my sister's murderer. I won't stop until I find him. Somehow, you're important. That's why you're staying with me. Call it kidnapping if you want. I don't care. If I hadn't shown up when I did, you'd be dead right now."

"I still don't know how I can help." He scratched the back of his head and then folded his arms as if they were talking about something as mundane as the weather. He looked bored.

"I don't either, but we will soon enough. Now, we will see someone who can help us or at least give us a direction to go in. He has a history of finding people and investigative work. In the meantime, don't try anything stupid. I need you to stay with me a little while longer. This isn't going to be like in the movies. I'm not going to hold a gun on you the whole time. But if you try to escape, you'll regret it. You're my pet until this thing is over. Are we clear?"

Jack nodded and stared out the dark windshield.

"Good. The last four years have been hard. I've been through a lot—kidnapped, stabbed, shot at, and almost killed numerous times. It pisses a girl off. Don't add to my list of woes. Be quiet and be cool, and everything will work out."

Jack turned and met her eyes. She could almost see the confusion on his face. But it might have been something deeper, like an understanding, a knowing. Then he glanced away.

"I've seen a lot of dead girls in my time," he said after a moment. "I've also been shot." He pointed at the scar on his head. "I can help as I know how cops think. A certain part of my analytical mind came back over the years." He turned back to her. "When I was a cop, I worked homicide. We investigated the kind of murderer you're looking for. I might have even worked on your sister's case, but I don't know because I've spent so many years trying to learn how to live again." He paused and twisted in his seat. "I will say one thing, though, the name Vivian Roberts rings a bell."

Chapter 8

Officer Parkman set his coffee down without spilling it. Some days were better than others. Parkman was on his fourth coffee and his seventh toothpick. He figured chewing the little pieces of wood would kill him one day, but he just couldn't stop.

Sarah Roberts.

He had tried to keep tabs on her over the years since her kidnapping, but she remained too elusive. He interviewed her parents and her few friends and even tried to talk to her directly, but she avoided cops. He couldn't blame her, especially after what happened four years ago.

Sarah had popped up in the news many times since then. There was never any proof of intent with her. She would show up at crime scenes. She would stop a crime from happening, then disappear. Once, she even walked ten people out of a burning building unscathed. No one knew how she got inside the building in the first place.

Parkman was there that night. It was an old five-story

printing company building. The company had gone bankrupt in the early 90s. The building's main floor was being used for the weekly meetings of a writer's group. The group had planned a Halloween party. All the members were supposed to walk through the abandoned floors above while people already in place would scare the ink out of them. While that was going on, the president of the writer's group started a small fire to act out a pyromania skit from his new short story. The fire spread fast, and by the time smoke reached the fifth floor, the twenty people up there could only get down to the third floor.

According to their combined statements, Sarah had been waiting on the third floor. She used an ax to chip away at an old boarded-up window. The folding ladder she had brought with her was secured to the ledge, and everyone climbed out with five minutes to spare before parts of the ladder were consumed by fire.

The authorities picked her up for questioning after that one. They wanted to know how she got into the building and why she knew to bring the ax and the ladder. His fellow officers interviewed her and drilled questions into her somber face but got nowhere. She had committed no crime, so they had to let her go. She told them that if she were gifted, she would hardly have allowed herself to be kidnapped, beaten, and almost killed all those years ago. "Come on, think about it," was all she would say.

Parkman's work had suffered because of Sarah Roberts. Two years ago, he worried that his obsession with her would cost him his job. After repeated warnings about his conduct regarding the Roberts family, Parkman capitulated.

Yet now, her name had resurfaced. This time in a more

serious way. An anonymous tip said that Sarah shot the guy found in Jack Tate's house. The knife used to kill the man was Jack's kitchen knife, and Jack Tate had been at the police station earlier in the evening. He was actually in police custody not an hour before all this went down. He had supposedly found a dead body buried ten minutes from his front door. Parkman had already figured out that the rips in the shirts tied it all together, but nothing else made sense.

Parkman believed it had everything to do with Sarah. If she truly had shot the guy, there had to be a reason. If he knew anything about Sarah, he knew she wasn't a criminal. In his mind, she was a superhero. That wasn't the sentiment his colleagues used. No, their words were harsher, cruder. Some wanted to bring her down, hinting that she set accidents up just to save people. He even overheard others whisper occult stuff, like she's possessed because she knows the future.

Whatever they believed, Parkman knew he was her only friend inside the police department. This meant he needed to locate her before anyone else did.

With the shooting from last night on record and Sarah as the person of interest, she could go down hard.

He drank the rest of his coffee, tossed the paper cup in the trash, and headed for his car. He popped a fresh toothpick into his mouth as he stepped outside.

It was six a.m.

Time to find Sarah Roberts and Jack Tate.

And he knew just the person to talk to.

Dolan Ryan.

Chapter 9

"COME IN, COME IN," Dolan squinted in the morning sun as he opened the door. "You must be Jack Tate."

Jack looked at him sideways. "How do you know my name?"

"He's psychic," Sarah said.

"I saw it on the news." Dolan looked at Sarah. "Both your names were mentioned."

They moved out of the foyer and into Dolan's kitchen.

"Coffee, anyone?" he asked.

Jack and Sarah shook their heads in unison. Dolan leaned against the counter and waited as they sat at his kitchen table. He saw that Sarah was cautious around Jack, watching him. There was a bump in her shirt near her belt line where a gun was hidden. Sarah wasn't taking any chances.

Sarah told Dolan everything that had happened in the last twelve hours, starting with her premonition and Jack finding the girl's body in the woods, until they arrived at Dolan's.

Dolan glanced at Jack. "You don't know who those guys

were?"

Jack shook his head. "I've got enemies from a few decades ago. I'm in my mid-sixties, retired for a long time on a disability pension. If it was from my past, they might as well give up. I'll die of natural causes soon enough."

Dolan looked at Sarah without acknowledging the attempt at humor. He noticed right away that something was happening to her. "Are you okay?"

Sarah grabbed a notebook from her back pocket and slipped off the chair. She hit the floor, her body as limp as if she was syrup poured from a bottle. Her eyes rotated back in her head. She gripped the pen so tight Dolan thought she might snap it in two.

From the angle Dolan had, he couldn't see what she was writing. Jack leaned away from them, an expression of surprise on his face.

A moment later, Sarah gasped and sat up. She used the chair to get herself off the floor.

"What does it say?" Dolan asked, moving closer.

Sarah looked down at what she had written, her eyes widening. "It says, *run out the front door ... they're in the back.*"

"Then let's go!" Dolan said as he jumped into action. He grabbed Jack's arm to get him up from his chair.

Dolan got to the front door first and peeked outside. The morning sun bounced off parked cars and glinted in windows, but he saw no movement. As he gripped the door handle, the soft sound of glass breaking somewhere in the back of the house chilled him. He ripped the door open, and all three of them tumbled onto Dolan's front porch and right into Officer Parkman.

"Whoa," Parkman said. Dolan saw him flip a toothpick to the other side of his mouth before he asked, "Where are you three going so fast?"

How did I not see him standing there?

"Someone just broke a window at the back of my house. We're assuming they're armed and dangerous."

Parkman flipped open his holster. In a calm voice, he said, "Quietly run across the lawn and get into my cruiser. Wait for me there."

Dolan nodded and started away, staying ahead of Jack and Sarah, who followed close behind. He looked back once and saw Parkman talking into a cell phone. Then Parkman lowered into a crouch and jumped through Dolan's front door. Dolan remembered Parkman from a couple of years ago. He had harassed him about Sarah, trying to get information on her.

The trio made it to the police car and then ran past it.

"Aren't we supposed to wait inside?" Jack asked.

"You go inside that cop car, you'll die," Dolan said.

Sarah nodded. "I'd listen to him."

They ran across the street and behind a black van. From this vantage point, they could securely watch the front of Dolan's house.

Gunfire erupted from inside his house. It always surprised him how much it sounded like firecrackers. He looked at the houses immediately in front of them. Everything was still and quiet. He looked back to his house. Parkman had reappeared. He was hunched down at the end of the porch behind a lounge chair. Sirens sounded in the distance.

"What do we do now?" Sarah asked.

Dolan looked back at her. "I think you'll have to trust the police on this one."

Sarah stared back at him. "Never."

"You need to think about that."

"Just did."

"Look, you can't help anybody if you're dead."

"I won't be dead. Vivian would not lead me to my own death."

"You don't know that. What if she gets selfish and decides to have you join her? You almost died four years ago. It was only luck that you lived. It had nothing to do with Vivian."

Sarah scanned the street to determine which way the sirens were coming from.

"Come on, Jack, we're leaving." She pulled on Jack's sleeve.

"Where will you go?" Dolan asked.

"Off the grid until my sister lets me in on what's happening."

Dolan surrendered. "Be safe, and call me if you need me."

Sarah bent low and motioned for Jack to do it, too. They hustled across the street and into Sarah's car. Dolan watched her do a U-turn and drive north as three cruisers came in from the south.

It took ten minutes for the police to confirm all suspects were gone, except for the one shot by Officer Parkman. The perp had died on Dolan's hallway runner.

Dolan was giving his statement to another officer when Parkman interrupted.

"We found these on the dead guy. Any idea why?"

He pushed photos into Dolan's hand. They were a little bigger than wallet size. Just big enough to carry in a breast pocket. Sarah was in the first shot. It was a bad picture taken about four or five years ago when she looked like a cancer patient with all her hair missing. The second shot was of him. It was not a flattering one, either. It reminded him of his passport photo, also taken about five years ago when he used to do all those psychic fairs in various cities.

The people in the third, fourth, and fifth photos he didn't recognize.

"Who are these three shots of?"

"That one there," Parkman moved closer and pointed, "is the dead girl Jack Tate found last night. The other two we're still trying to identify. How do you think Jack is tied into all this? And if he is, how safe is Sarah right now? I'd also like to know why they ran after I told all three of you to wait in my cruiser."

"You know as well as I do that Sarah doesn't trust cops."

"We may be her only friends right now. As it stands, we want to question her about the shooting in front of Jack Tate's house earlier tonight. There's a reason people run from the police, Dolan. I may be a cop, but I also care about Sarah's safety, whether she knows it or not."

"I can attest that Sarah isn't running from you in the traditional sense. She knows what she's doing. She's tough." He handed the pictures back as another plainclothes cop burst into the front door.

"Thought you might want to know this."

Parkman turned toward him and pulled the toothpick out of his mouth. "What is it?"

"I think we've got the connection to Jack Tate," the cop

said as he flipped the papers back and forth.

"Come on, come on, what is it?" Parkman asked.

"About twenty years ago, the last case Tate worked was a cold case."

"So, how is that connected to this?" He tossed the mangled pick in Dolan's kitchen sink.

"A girl was raped and murdered. Tate was shot in the head, presumably by the murderer."

"Would I know this case?" Parkman asked.

The cop nodded. "The murder victim was Vivian Roberts. Sarah Robert's sister."

Chapter 10

Sarah drove over two hours until they reached the next city. It didn't look good to be running, but she had no choice. She had gone to Dolan for help and somehow drew the killers there.

She needed to get a handle on what was going on without risking the welfare of others.

Jack had fallen asleep and slept quietly beside her. She kept the radio on low but heard nothing new on the news.

A restaurant came up on her right, offering an all-you-can-eat breakfast. She pulled in, turned the car off, and put her head back.

***

She must have fallen asleep. The clock on the dash said she had lost two hours. Jack sat on the hood of the Kia.

The door opened with a squeak when she got out to stretch her legs.

"Why didn't you leave?" she asked.

He turned around. "Because I remembered the connection. Ever since you told me your sister's name, it's been stuck in my head. Vivian Roberts was the last case I worked on before I got shot."

Instantly awake, Sarah walked around the car and stood before him.

"So you *are* part of this. That means whoever shot you all those years ago is connected, too, and they wanted to silence you as you were probably getting close to them."

Jack nodded.

A large truck eased past them. It lumbered by slowly but was so loud they stopped talking until it passed. Sarah turned to avoid the small amount of dust that floated by as the truck passed.

"You're in more trouble than you think," Jack said.

"I know, but what about you? Those men were sent to kill you last night."

"Somehow, because of who you are or what you're doing, they've decided that I need to be taken care of. Maybe whoever shot me twenty years ago wants to finish the job. I had lost my memory, but now things have changed." He paused and wiped his face with his hand. "People you know or have worked with before are in danger. Just look what happened at Dolan's house this morning."

It still didn't add up. Why hadn't Vivian given her more to work with? This wasn't normal. Sarah liked when a message came through, and then she acted on it and was done with it. The messages were more like riddles whenever prophecies had something to do with family. It was left for her to figure out on her own. This was the only part of her ability as an automatic writer that she hated because it came with the potential for personal injury. If this ultimately led to her sister's murderer, she would do whatever was needed. A man like that couldn't be allowed to remain free.

"Let's get some food and get back on the road," Sarah said.

After they ate and used the facilities, they ordered two large coffees and left the truck stop, heading back into town.

Sarah pulled out her cell phone and tried her parents' home number. She got no answer. If someone was after her and went to Dolan's, they may try her parents next. Hopefully, they were just out shopping or having lunch with a friend.

She tried Esmerelda next. The line was picked up on the first ring.

"Hi, Esmerelda, how are you? Is everything okay there?"

"Hello, Sarah. Everything seems fine. Is there something I should know?"

She came right out and said it. Esmerelda wouldn't have it any other way. She told her what happened the previous evening and finished with the incident at Dolan's place this morning.

"I tried my parents but got no answer. You need to be careful. I don't know who these people are or what they're capable of, but they could be coming after people I know."

"I'll try to call your mom and dad, too. I'll head to their place if I can't raise them."

"Okay, thanks, and I'll call you as soon as I hear something."

She hung up and watched the road. What was her next move? The cops were looking for them because of the shooting at Jack's place last night. Jack found a dead body, and now he's missing. Parkman saw them together earlier this morning at Dolan's. She wasn't a fugitive, but she couldn't see how being on the run from the cops would help her solve this current problem. But being in custody would not help either.

That left only Parkman.

What was he doing at Dolan's this morning, anyway?

She scrolled through the phone book on her cell phone and stopped at Parkman's number. He'd called so often in the past she had kept his number, so she knew when *not* to answer.

She squinted into the sun and took a sip of her coffee.

She hit send and waited.

"Parkman here."

"It's Sarah."

"Where are you?"

"Out of town."

"Why are you calling me?" Parkman asked.

"Because you're the only cop I think I can trust and because you would know that I didn't kill anybody last night at Jack Tate's home."

She felt Jack's eyes on her. She watched the road and kept the phone pressed to her ear, ignoring him.

"If what you say about trusting me is true, why have you been avoiding me all these years? I could've helped."

"Parkman, you were bothering me. You called my friends and family all the time. You acted like a stalker. I know you figured out enough about me to realize that I'm not responsible for what happened in the last twelve hours. You know I'm clean. That's why I'm calling you."

"You're too late."

"What are you talking about?"

"They put me on a desk. I've got a week's worth of paperwork for the shooting at Dolan's, and then, until this is over with you, my boss said I'd be at a desk. I think they're afraid it's too personal for me."

"Is it?" Sarah asked.

"Yes, I suppose it is. What are you going to do? They have your name on every cruiser. They're looking for you hardcore, and you know why? Because they don't understand you as I do."

"Can you tell me who was at Jack's place last night or at Dolan's this morning? Do you guys know yet?"

"No. They didn't give me the ID on the body they pulled from Jack's foyer, and they yanked me before forensics dealt with the body at Dolan's. I'm out of the loop on this."

"Okay, call me if you think I need to know something," Sarah said and made to hang up. She paused as she heard Parkman screaming for her to wait.

With the phone back at her ear, Sarah asked, "What is it?"

"Have you still got Jack Tate with you?"

"Yes." She snuck a look at him. He was sipping his coffee and staring out the window.

"Did you know he used to be a cop?"

"Yes."

"His last case was your sister's murder."

"I know."

"I guess you would. That's why you showed up at his house last night. Well, I have something else for you."

"What?"

"He was under investigation a couple of times as a police officer for conduct unbecoming. Also, he had a younger brother who was killed four years ago. As far as I know, they never spoke again after Jack got shot all those years ago. I think you'd know Jack's younger brother."

"Really? Who was he?"

"A man named Alex Stuart. It's the same Alex that kidnapped you four years ago. You remember Dolan's old assistant at the psychic fair. The same guy who hired Gert and his brother, Matt, to kidnap teenage girls for money."

Sarah couldn't believe what Parkman was telling her. How could everything be so connected? She stole another glance at Jack. He didn't seem to notice her.

"You're kidding, right? Tell me you're kidding."

"I'm not. I read Jack Tate's file a year ago while researching you. I know him and his career because he was the guy who almost collared your sister's murderer. Watch yourself, Sarah. He may not be the good guy you think he is."

Chapter 11

IT WAS JUST AFTER noon when she pulled onto her parents' street. She parked ten houses away and got out.

"Jack, we need to change cars. I'm not a thief, and I don't have the kind of money to just go and buy one. That's why we're here. My parents live on this street. We're going to quietly walk up and knock on the front door like ordinary people. Okay?"

Jack nodded. "Did you call first? Are they expecting us?"

"I called, but no one answered."

Jack gave her a look that said *be careful*. She nodded, and together they started up the street. It was a short walk in a neighborhood where nothing ever changed. She'd lived here for many years. Shortly after her kidnapping four years ago, her parents almost split up, and she had to move out as they proved quite hard to live with. She was turning nineteen then, and the rules they imposed on her were for a ten-year-old. They'd made it through the tough time, though, and were recently doing well as far as she could tell.

Her cell phone rang on the front steps of her parents' house. She read the screen. It said *private caller*, which meant it was probably the police. She chose to ignore it.

Jack looked like he was right at home in his role as playing a cop again. He stared across the street and into the eyes of drivers going by. She couldn't trust him, but he might be good to have around for now.

"Come on," she said and started up the front walkway.

The house felt sad. There was something dismal about it. Perhaps she just missed being here. She glanced at the window that opened into what used to be her bedroom and longed for an earlier time when things were simpler.

When she tapped the doorbell, she heard it ring on the inside. Jack continued to watch the street, intently staring at a certain house.

"What's going on, Jack?" she asked. "You see something?"

"I thought I saw someone watching us through those curtains in that house," he said, nodding to show her which one. "Do you know who lives there?"

"The beige house with that overhang by the porch?"

"Yeah."

"That's the Ellis's house. They wouldn't be watching us. They would've come out and said hello if they saw me."

Sarah hit the doorbell again. Her cell phone rang. Call display said it was private, just like the call from moments ago.

Jack moved up the sidewalk toward her. "Can we go around to the back door?" he asked.

"Sure. Why?"

"Something's wrong across the street. Aren't you going

to answer your phone?"

They started moving to the back of the house as Sarah answered her phone and put it to her ear.

"I know you're there. We have a problem. You have what I need, and I have what you need."

"Who is this?" Sarah asked. Jack walked ahead of her and banged on the house's back door.

"That's not important. But what is of great *fucking* importance is Jack Tate."

"Why?" Sarah tried to keep her anger in check. Her life as an automatic writer and its mysterious messages was something she dealt with, but when people *acted* mysterious, it pissed her off.

"I'm ready to do an exchange. Your parents for Jack Tate."

"My parents? How's that?" Sarah asked as her stomach dropped. She joined Jack in banging on the back door.

"If it weren't broad daylight, we would take him right now. I saw you walk up to your parents' house with Jack. They're not there. You're wasting your time."

Sarah pulled the phone from her ear and covered the mouthpiece. "Jack, you were right," she whispered. "We're being watched. Let's move."

They jumped off the porch and raced to the back fence. Before passing through the gate, Sarah tried to listen to her phone again. The caller had hung up.

She dropped the phone in her pocket and jumped the fence.

Could my parents have been kidnapped?

How could she live with herself if something happened to them?

"What was the call about?" Jack asked.

"The guy on the phone wants to exchange you for my parents," she said. Tears crept into her vision. She didn't want to cry. This was not a good time to be crying. "They were watching us like you said."

"Call the police and tell them what you know. Maybe they can do something about the people in the Ellis's house."

Sarah pulled out her cell phone and went to dial 911 but stopped. She scrolled through her last number redials and called Parkman instead.

"Parkman here."

They emerged from the alley and turned left, walking away from her car. "We have a problem."

"What kind of problem?" Parkman asked.

"It looks like whoever is behind all this has kidnapped my parents. They just called me and asked for Jack in exchange. They were watching us from across the street."

"Watching you? Where are you?"

"At my parents' house."

"I knew people close to you would be in danger," Parkman said as if talking to himself. "Damn."

"You win the prize. Now, can we get someone on this? Who are these people? They have my parents. This isn't working out well. If anything happens to them, I will be seriously pissed off."

"Okay, I'll look into it. But once I pass on the information, they'll put me back at my desk."

"Fine, but Parkman, do something. I need your help." Sarah hung up. She hoped that putting her trust in a cop wouldn't backfire.

"What now?" Jack asked. "The cops are looking for both

of us. Whoever is behind this sent goons to my house last night to kill me, then they went to Dolan's, and now your parents are missing. This means they're well prepared and serious, and *that* leaves me with one conclusion."

Sarah looked over at him as they ran down the street. "What conclusion is that?"

"I'm the one they're after because they believe I can identify them. Since you saved my life last night and whisked me away, they're going after you now."

"It's deeper than that. You and my family are much closer than you think."

Jack slowed and looked at her. "What are you talking about?"

"Come on. We can't stop," she said as she tugged his arm and continued down the street.

"How are we connected?" Jack asked.

"Your brother, Alex, had me kidnapped four years ago."

Jack stopped walking. He raised a hand to the side of his head.

"What?" Sarah asked.

"That must be it."

"What?" she asked again and tossed both hands in the air to express her frustration.

"It's a long story, but I'll try to make it quick. My family was always on the wrong side of the law. I hated it. That's why I became a cop. I had a brother named Alex. He was born twenty years after my sister and me but to a different father."

"Okay, great story, but we need to keep moving. I want some distance from whoever was watching us. Tell me more on the way."

They started walking again.

"Keep talking. What else is there?" She was missing something, and if she didn't figure it out soon, people would start dying.

"When you said it was my brother who kidnapped you four years ago, it suddenly hit me."

"What hit you? This is getting frustrating. Do I have to pull it out of you?"

He looked at her. She could tell he wasn't used to a twenty-two-year-old being so demanding.

Well, he'd better get fucking used to it.

"I'm not taking my time on purpose. Gathering my memories is a chore after a bullet erased most of them. Give me a second …"

A car traveled up the street too fast. It aimed toward them. Sarah pushed Jack back and started away from the sidewalk. The car pulled over, kicking up gravel and dust. The passenger door swung open, and Sarah bent to look in, her hand ready to yank her weapon out.

"Get in!" Esmerelda shouted.

Sarah released her grip on the butt of her gun and hopped in the back seat. Jack jumped in beside her.

"You okay?" Esmerelda asked.

"Better now," Sarah nodded. "Why are you here?"

Esmerelda looked at her in the rearview mirror as she got the car back on the road. "I told you I'd check on your parents. When I didn't get an answer, I came over and saw people watching their house from across the street. I was on the opposite end of the street when I saw you walking up to knock on the front door. Then I saw you two heading around to the back of the house. I had to drive over a few blocks until I found you. You want to introduce me to your new friend?"

"His name is Jack Tate, and he's mixed up in all this. He's an ex-cop and was just about to tell me something interesting about his family history."

Jack looked at her and then at the back of Esmerelda's head. He appeared dazed. "It all started when I left home to join the police force. My mother got mixed up in voodoo. The man she met was crazy. He got her pregnant, and she had Alex Stuart. His last name is different from mine because of the different fathers."

Esmerelda cut in. "Do you mean the same Alex who was Dolan's assistant? The one I used to work with at the psychic fair?"

"Yes, I do. After he was born, I only visited the house once in a while. I wasn't around much, so I wasn't privy to all the abuse. I remember one night, I came over unannounced in my cruiser. This would've been when Alex was eight years old or so. They were doing some kind of ritual with candles in the living room. I asked what had happened to them when I saw that Alex was naked. I arrested Armond Stuart, Alex's father, on various child abuse charges. He got bail and was home the next day, and *I* was told to stay away. My own mother didn't want anything to do with me. This ritual stuff blinded her. The investigators came up with all kinds of insane and stupid stuff Armond was doing."

Sarah turned in her seat. "So what came of it?"

"Armond was convicted and imprisoned until Alex was fifteen years old. My mother disowned me."

"Sad story, but how is it relevant to the here and now?" Esmerelda asked.

Jack looked out the window at the buildings going by. Sarah saw him rubbing the rip in his shirt. "Alex was really messed up. We bumped into each other occasionally. I wanted to keep tabs on my mother, you know, see how she was doing. Alex was happy his dad was in jail. So we talked. One day he would talk about voodoo dolls, and then he'd talk about out-of-body experiences. He always smelled of cologne, like he was showering in the stuff."

Esmerelda and Sarah exchanged a look of understanding in the rearview mirror.

"Alex was sexually and physically abused," Jack continued. "He was quite sick himself. He got involved in fake psychics ripping people off. The last I heard, he was involved with the psychic fair. I remember checking them out in my spare time about six years ago. It seemed like a good deal for him as his boss, who I remember now was Dolan, helped the police to locate missing children. I later heard Alex was killed in a shootout somewhere in the Midwest."

Sarah nodded. "I was there." She chose to spare Jack the details that she had killed Alex in the most brutal way by tearing off part of his face with a rusty nail. "Is there anything else?"

Jack looked at her, his facial muscles twitching. "After Alex died, I decided to see what Armond was up to. I discovered that he was mixed up in the business Alex was into. All I could gather was a few teenage girls didn't make it home. They were sexually abused and killed. The police attributed those crimes to Alex after he died, but I felt it had something to do with Armond because they found a voodoo doll with one of the bodies. I told the police about it, but they brushed me off. The case was closed and filed. I was quite interested because my last case was Vivian, and we know what happened to her." Jack looked down at the rip in his shirt. "Armond is still out there. He'd be about sixty now. I think Armond shot me, but I have no proof."

"Sarah, here, take this." Esmerelda reached across to the passenger seat and picked something up. She handed Sarah a notebook and a pen.

"You're going to need that to help us get out of this."

Chapter 12

DOLAN WATCHED AS THE glass repairman set a new pane in place. The police had left an hour ago.

He paced to show the guy how antsy he was. Because a shooting had taken place, the Special Investigations Unit had come in to examine the area. Dolan had called the glass repairman, but all SIU let the repairman do was measure the window and leave. Not until the cops were through would they let him replace the window.

"How much longer?" Dolan asked.

"Five minutes."

Dolan grabbed the kitchen phone and dialed. He got a receptionist and then was put through.

"Sam Johnson."

"Sam, it's Dolan."

"How are things? It's been a long time. Last I heard, you'd retired from the psychic fair business."

Dolan moved to the kitchen and sat on one of the chairs. "Sam, something has come up, and I need your help." Dolan waited at least ten seconds and then asked, "Are you still there?"

"Yes." Another pause. "You know what happened the last time I helped you four years ago? I almost bought a ticket out of here. They've had me running the evidence room ever since."

"That's not entirely true, and you know it. You were a cop doing your job. We worked together, and mistakes were made. I was shot, too …" Dolan drifted off as he saw the glass repairman getting up and looking at him. "One sec, Sam."

He put a hand on the phone. "Are you done?"

"Yes. I'll collect my tools and leave."

Dolan nodded and went back to the phone. "Sam, it's about Sarah."

"Oh, and that inspires me to help even more," Sam said.

"She's mixed up in something and needs our help. You know she has a problem with cops, but she'll trust you. After what you and I did for her four years ago, she would be happy to have you on board."

"Look, Dolan, leave me out. I live an easy life now. I sit in the evidence room all day and go home to a quiet evening by the television. I golf, too. I used to be young and naïve, but not anymore. That isn't my life."

"Sam, listen to yourself. Sarah is in trouble. She's on the run with an ex-cop named Jack Tate. She showed up here this morning, and we were attacked at my house. That nosy cop, Parkman, showed up at the right time. He shot the perp. I've had time to think about this. Whoever they are, they're going after people close to Sarah. They know where she'll turn next and who she'll turn to. We need you. Sarah needs you."

"Sorry, Dolan, I can't. With all due respect, try some of your psychic stuff on this and inform the proper authorities. I can't help."

Dolan bowed his head. He heard the front door shut as the glass repairman left.

"Will you at least call me if you hear anything from your colleagues?"

Silence again. Then, "I will call. But the chances of me hearing something are slim to none. Dolan, I'm down in the evidence locker. I never hear about a case unless they bring me the evidence."

"What happened to you, Sam? We used to work together. How many cases did we see through to the end? I'm a friend. I need your help. You're the only one I would ask."

"At any other time in our history, you know I would be there, but I was shot and left for dead. If Alex's bullet had been a little to the left or a little to the right, I'd be dead and rotting at this minute. Think of it like a skydiver; your parachute doesn't open on a dive. Somehow you hit trees and finally the roof of a barn, and then you flop to the ground. You almost die, but the trees break your fall. After a lengthy hospital stay, you commit to never dive again. That's me. I don't go in the field. I *won't* go in the field."

"Just call me if you hear anything," Dolan said and hung up without saying goodbye.

Chapter 13

"Where are we going?" Sarah asked.

Esmerelda merged onto a two-lane highway and sped up. She checked her rearview mirror more than once.

"Is everything okay?" Sarah asked as she turned around and looked out the back window. She only saw a line of cars fading away as they went faster.

"I think we're being followed," Esmerelda said. "It's probably the people who were watching your house. They would have tried to locate you as I did. Maybe they saw you get in my car."

"What are they driving?" Sarah asked.

"It looked like a large black SUV. They're about eight cars back. They've taken every turn I have."

"Aren't we going too fast for this highway?" Jack asked.

"Probably. But I need to get some distance between—oh shit!" Esmerelda smacked the steering wheel.

Sarah looked up ahead. A police officer stepped onto the road and waved Esmerelda to pull over. They were still a hundred yards away, but Sarah could already see the radar gun on a tripod and the front grill of a police cruiser.

"It's okay, Esmerelda. Whoever is following us will get spooked away by the cops, and the worst we'll get is a speeding ticket."

"I wouldn't be so sure. What if this traffic cop recognizes one of you two?"

She eased the car over and slowed to a stop as far from the road as she could. The officer walked up to the driver's side window. Esmerelda rolled it down slowly while watching her mirrors. Sarah turned around to look through the back window. Car after car passed by, but no SUV.

"Do you know how fast you were going, ma'am?" The cop leaned down to talk to Esmerelda.

"Not really, Officer. I kinda got carried away. We were talking, and after I merged, I accelerated and didn't focus enough on the speed. Sorry about that."

Esmerelda was in her sixties. The cop, however, wasn't buying the brand of old-woman sympathy she was trying to sell him. He looked through her window and into the back seat.

"I'm going to need to see your driver's license and registration, ma'am."

Esmerelda fumbled in the glove box and produced what the cop wanted. He asked her to wait for him as he returned to the cruiser. Sarah kept an eye on the road. Jack sat beside her, fumbling with the rip in his shirt.

What the hell is it with that damn rip?

"There's a problem," Esmerelda said.

"What problem?" Sarah asked.

"I don't know yet, but there is. He's got another cop with

him. They're both in their cruiser talking. The cop who took my license keeps looking up at us."

"It's routine. Nothing to worry about," Jack said.

A black SUV slowed down to park on the shoulder about two-hundred yards back.

"Esmerelda, look behind us," Sarah said. "Is that the SUV you saw?"

Esmerelda turned to look out the back window. "Who could they possibly be?"

The cop opened his door and stepped from the cruiser. He placed a hand on his holster as he neared Esmerelda's vehicle.

"What's the plan?" Sarah asked as she reached back and touched her gun. She had no idea what this cop was up to.

"I have no clue," Esmerelda said.

But Esmerelda's words were lost to her as Sarah blacked out.

***

Sarah swam back to consciousness, unsure how long she'd been out. The pen Esmerelda had given her was locked in her hand. Before reading the message in the notebook, she looked up at the officer who shouted through Esmerelda's window.

"I'm asking you to step out of the vehicle," he said.

"Okay," Esmerelda said. "I will, Officer, but I want to know why?"

The cop unclipped his holster. His partner came around the front of the vehicle.

"I have reason to believe you are aiding and abetting two

people wanted in connection with a shooting. I need you to exit the vehicle and keep your hands where I can see them."

Esmerelda reached for the door and asked under her breath, "Are you okay, Sarah?"

Esmerelda got out of the car before Sarah could respond. Jack stood beside the car, too. Both doors remained open. A vehicle raced by, the wind subtly shaking Esmerelda's car.

"I won't ask you again," the cop leaned down and said to Sarah.

Sarah edged to the door but remained inside the vehicle. "Officer, can I ask you something?"

"No. Get out of the vehicle, now."

"Do you know a man named Aaron Beck?"

The cop looked at his partner, then back at Sarah.

"Yes, I do. He's a close friend of mine. How do you know him? What's Aaron got to do with this?"

"Did he tell you what happened on Front Street with his wife, Carol, a few days ago?"

"What are you talking about?"

Sarah placed her feet on the gravel shoulder outside the car and looked up at him. "I'm telling you this because I want you to trust us. That woman there is a renowned psychic. This man here, Jake Tate, is a retired police officer …"

The cop cut in. "I know all of you, and we're supposed to take you in, Sarah Roberts. That is your name, right?"

"I'm the girl from the bus that spoke to Aaron and told him to call his wife so she wouldn't get killed by that truck."

Something she said hit a nerve. Both cops looked at each other, then back at her.

"Here's why I'm telling you this," she said. "If we do not

get back on the highway within a few minutes, you and your partner will be killed."

His hand returned to a spot on his belt where he removed his pepper spray canister.

"Okay, enough fooling around. Get out of the *fucking* car. We have a job to do, and that job is taking you in right now."

Sarah stood slowly and looked back at the idling SUV. It hadn't moved yet.

She raised her hands above her head, the notebook in her left. She glanced up at it and started reading.

"Officer Cooper. You've been on the force for eight years. Your wife, Sofia, has asked you to consider another career as she fears for your safety." Sarah stopped to let that sink in. "Mr. Cooper, we are being tailed by highly professional people who will stop at nothing to get what they want. I know it sounds over the top, but it's true. They kidnapped my parents and followed us when you pulled our car over. There's an SUV about two-hundred yards back parked on the shoulder. Those are the people responsible for the shooting last night and this morning. We also believe those are the people responsible for the dead body Mr. Tate found last night in the woods."

Officer Cooper stared at her. He still held the pepper spray in his hand. His partner had not drawn a weapon. While Sarah spoke, he had taken a quick look back at the SUV.

"Whatever your story is, you can tell it to the cop who takes your statement," Cooper said. "My job is to take you in. But I'm curious, how did you know all that stuff about me?"

"It's written right here. I'm an automatic writer. I write things that someone on the Other Side channels through me. They just gave me this information to show you how real this is, so when I say that you could be killed if you don't let us go. It's not a threat. It's the truth."

"I'm taking it as a threat. Give me that notebook," he said and grabbed it from Sarah's hand. "I want all of you down, on the ground. Now!"

Esmerelda and Jack started to get down, but Sarah remained standing.

"You're not listening, Officer Cooper. We don't have the time—"

"*You're* not listening. On the ground, now, or I will spray you."

Sarah started to drop, keeping the gun at her back hidden. She glanced behind them and saw the SUV moving. It was merging with traffic heading their way.

Cooper's partner worked on securing Esmerelda's hands and then stood and started securing Jack's. Officer Cooper had returned his weapon to his holster.

"That SUV is coming," Sarah said. "Please, I implore you. Pull your gun back out and get behind the vehicle."

He wasn't listening. He read out loud from the notebook, "*They're like a sect or a cult. They're meaner and more organized and enjoy the hunt and the kill. Beware of Armond. He's cunning.* What is this stuff? Are you serious? Were you referring to cops when you wrote this, too? And who is Armond? Hey, Joe, do you know anyone named *Armond*?"

The other cop shook his head as he finished with Jack's wrists.

"Get away from that SUV. Now!" Sarah yelled.

Esmerelda dropped to her knees and started around to the front of her car. Jack didn't move. Before she rolled away toward the back, she saw Cooper and his partner turn to address the SUV as it slowed.

"Move along. No show here," Cooper shouted.

Then he yelled the word *gun*. She heard bullets hitting metal as they embedded themselves into the side of Esmerelda's car. Instinctively, she ducked her head and rolled away.

Doors opened and closed. A large man grabbed her arm and half lifted, half dragged her to the SUV, his grip unforgiving. Esmerelda and Jack were already being tucked away inside by other armed men. Before the last man got in the SUV, he turned and emptied his gun into the two policemen who lay on the shoulder of the road.

Cooper's body spasmed as each bullet hit him.

She eased out her gun and aimed it at the guy. As professional as they were, she was surprised they hadn't frisked her.

Her aim was true. She had two bullets left, and both hit him in the back of the head. He went down like a heavy bag of rocks.

She addressed the driver, but he had already drawn on her.

"Drop it, or you die," he said.

Her gun was empty. She needed to decide whether to bluff or drop her weapon in the second or two she had.

As it turned out, the driver was a bit of a marksman. He fired his weapon, and the next instant, Sarah's weapon tore out of her hand, landing on the shoulder of the road.

"Now, throw out your cell phone."

"I don't have it on me." Sarah tried to show a brave face to cover the lie, but the gun being shot out of her hand shook her up.

The driver adjusted his aim to the point where she saw directly down the barrel of the gun. "I won't ask again."

She pulled it out slowly. Like throwing a Frisbee, she tossed it away. The phone landed past the shoulder of the road in the tall grass.

A Plexiglas partition rose between the driver and the three prisoners. The backdoor window rose simultaneously.

Once all three of them were secure in the back of the SUV, Sarah tried the door, but it was locked. She kicked the door as the driver pulled back onto the highway.

Esmerelda asked her to stay calm. Save her energy. Wherever they were going, they would probably need it.

When Sarah glanced back to the parked cruiser and the three bodies, cars were already pulling over.

Her gun was left at the scene with her prints on it. Bullets from her gun were in the dead guy who shot the two cops.

Another manhunt would be on for her. This time, she wondered if she would make it out unscathed.

A feeling of peace came over her at having shot another human being. This time she had killed in cold blood and without hesitation. She felt a certain kind of pleasure in knowing that another piece of human scum had been wiped out.

Before this was over, a few more bottom feeders would need to die.

Chapter 14

Dolan got up and ran to answer his phone. He'd been waiting for a security guy to come by and give him an estimate on installing an alarm system.

"Hello."

"Dolan, we have a bigger problem than I thought."

"Sam," Dolan said, relieved. "I'm glad you called. What's going on?"

"Two traffic cops were killed this afternoon, and they found an unidentified body with the officers. Obviously, a full investigation will have to take place, but I'm hearing that the guy found on the side of the highway with the two dead cops had the same caliber gun as the guy found in Tate's house last night. But that's not all."

Dolan turned a kitchen chair away from the table and took a seat straddling it. "What else?"

"The unidentified guy had two bullets in the back of his head. It looks like they were fired from gun investigators found on site. Early ballistics suggests that it's the same gun used last night at Tate's house. I guess it's Sarah's weapon, and they'll find her prints on it."

Dolan ran a hand through his hair. "What could she possibly be mixed up in? She's usually helping people, not running around with guns and dead bodies. At least I can tell you she's not on the wrong side of the law."

"I know that, Dolan. But there's more."

"More?" Dolan asked. "Come on, Sam, what else?"

"Do you remember Sarah's parents, Caleb and Amelia?"

"Yes, I do."

"They've disappeared. Apparently, by the looks of the inside of their house, they've been kidnapped."

Dolan shot up from the kitchen chair and walked to the front door. He looked out into the street.

"How did this happen? How *could* this happen?"

"I have no idea, but I can tell you I'm pissed that two fellow officers are dead. Whoever did this will get caught. The police'll probably kill them before they're brought in, though."

"You know as well as I do that if these guys kill a cop, they won't bat an eye at killing Sarah."

"You mean Sarah and Esmerelda."

"What?" Dolan asked as he spun away from the door and started back to the kitchen. "You've got to be kidding me. How is Esmerelda mixed up in this?"

"It looks like the cops were doing a routine speed trap. They pulled Esmerelda's car over. She's missing, too. The officers radioed in that they had Esmerelda, Sarah, and Jack Tate, and they were bringing them in. That's all I got from upstairs on my lunch break."

"Sarah must've called Esmerelda for help just like she

called me. It almost feels like it didn't end four years ago." He paused and then said, "I'm coming over. Get off early. We've got to do something."

"There's not much we can do," Sam said.

Dolan made it to his bedroom. He ripped open drawers and started to get changed. "Yes, there is. We can find our friends, Sarah and Esmerelda. Have you heard if there were any witnesses to this shooting?"

"Responding officers are on the scene right now talking to the few people who pulled over and called it in on their cell phones."

"Okay, do what you can to find out what they're saying. I'll be there inside a half hour."

"Dolan, let me …"

Dolan terminated the call and stomped downstairs.

He walked into the main hallway to grab his car keys and was greeted by two men in black jackets.

They were holding guns.

Chapter 15

Sarah leaned against the back of the SUV, clenching her fists. When they opened the back door, she wanted to be ready.

"Sarah, the cop grabbed your notes and read something about a sect or cult. What was that?" Jack asked.

Sarah leaned back against the door. "I don't know, exactly. That's how the messages come through. Sometimes they're specific about a certain person or event. But when it comes to something I have to figure out, it's more of a riddle or just basic information. All I can assume is that the people responsible for all this are the sect the note referred to." Jack looked concerned. "What is it, Jack? Do you know something?" In his eyes, she detected something unsettling.

"I think I know what this is. There was even a warning about Armond, right?"

Sarah glanced at Esmerelda and then back at Jack. "Go on."

"Armond used to be involved in cults. After he served his

time in jail, he formed a following. They did harmless stuff on the surface, but I knew it had more to do with his sick desires. I think what happened to you and those other girls four years ago was Armond's brainchild, even though it looked like Alex was behind it. He was always trying to find a way to make money from his hallucinations."

"Could Armond be that powerful?" Esmerelda asked.

Jack nodded. "If left unchecked, yes. What I mean is, if he has been at this as long as I suspect with the police staying off his back, then he would have a large following and a group of insane people doing his bidding."

The driver pulled off the highway. Sarah looked out the back window trying to get a bearing on where they were but didn't recognize anything. They passed a sign, but she only got a glimpse of its backside.

"The fact that one person, a private citizen, could become so powerful is ridiculous," Sarah said. "What does this have to do with us?"

"Probably nothing," Jack said. "Wrong place at the wrong time. You said you got a message that those two men would kill me at my house last night?"

Sarah shook her head. "No, I received a message about my sister's murderer. It wasn't conclusive. It said I would find him, and it had your name and address. My goal last night was to question you to see how you were connected. I didn't know if you were her murderer or not. When I got to your house, you were downtown with the police. I sat across the street and waited. That's when I saw those men staking out your home, too. They broke into the back of that van, checked their weapons, and advanced on your house. One went in, and one waited outside for you. I interfered because you were the only name my sister gave me, and I had assumed they'd come to kill you."

Jack looked down at his lap. "You mean your dead sister? She's the one who talks to you, right?"

Sarah nodded. "It started five years ago."

Jack tilted his head and frowned. "Can you tell me how it started? What was your life like back then?"

She wondered how much to tell him. "I used to be depressed and a victim of trichotillomania, which means I used to be a puller."

"I feel dumb. What's a puller?"

"Someone who pulls their hair out strand by strand. It relieved the pain I felt on the inside. After what happened to me four years ago, I gained more self-esteem and found a way to stop pulling."

"Why would you do that in the first place?" Jack couldn't hide his expression of disgust.

"The operative word was *victim*. I didn't do it by choice. It was more than that. I *had* to. It was comforting. But I'm past that now."

The SUV slowed to a stop. They were in a wooded area with no visible buildings of any kind. The driver started up again and turned onto a dirt road.

Esmerelda asked him where they were going but got no response.

The SUV pulled into an opening about five hundred yards off the highway. Two other SUVs were parked in a small clearing, their backdoors open. Sarah counted four men wearing the same black jackets standing by their vehicles. It looked like they were holding handcuffs.

The SUV they were in stopped, and the driver got out.

"Okay, everyone, stay calm and do as they say," Sarah said.

"I agree," Jack said.

"If they wanted to kill us outright, they wouldn't have shown up with so many vehicles and handcuffs. That gives us time to figure something out."

The backdoor unlocked. Men walked toward the truck. They had guns in their hands. The driver of their SUV reached out to open the door.

"Easy now," he said and swung the door open so his cohorts could have a clear view. "Sarah, I want you first. Step out slowly and put these on," he tossed handcuffs at her. "You don't need to be told that if you make a sudden move, you'll get shot."

Esmerelda nodded at her. "It'll be okay, Sarah. Take care of yourself. Everything will work out."

"I'm sorry," Sarah said as she dropped to the ground and applied the cuffs to her wrists, keeping both arms in front. One of the men grabbed her by the hair. The pain was intense. She felt her knees weaken. The only thing that kept her upright was knowing that if her knees buckled, it would yank her hair more.

"I'm so angry I should fucking kill you right here and throw you in that ditch," the goon said. "You are such a meddling bitch. Do you know who's dead and lying in Tate's foyer? No, you don't. To you, he was just another bad guy. To us, he was a brother, you *fucking* whore."

"I didn't kill him," Sarah said. She thought her hair would separate from her scalp. Then the pressure was gone. Her peripheral vision saw his fist, but it was too late to do anything. Before it hit her cheek, she thanked God that he'd holstered his gun. The punch knocked her to the ground. With her hands cuffed and nothing but her elbows to break her fall, the other side of her face connected with the gravel on the shoulder of the road. A sharp, stinging rose immediately where a stone had torn her cheek.

For the past four years, she had saved people in scary situations and trained to be better with hand-to-hand combat and weapons. But she was surprised at how much that punch hurt. Her cheek felt double its normal size as the swelling started.

Someone grabbed her above the elbows. She was brought to a standing position.

"Please, she's a young girl," Esmerelda said. "Just leave her alone."

"Shut the fuck up, old lady or you're next."

The guy who punched her started to half walk, half drag her to one of the waiting SUVs. He opened the backdoor and shoved her in. She anticipated his move and got her legs up and in without banging them.

A long time had passed since she had felt this kind of pain. No amount of training had prepared her for the splitting headache she was going through as a result of getting her hair pulled, and face punched.

He grabbed her again and brought her close. He had a black blindfold in his hand. Just before he wrapped it around her head, she saw Esmerelda had been removed from the vehicle they had arrived in. They were walking her to the other SUV. Jack had remained in the original one.

Then a blindfold lowered over her eyes and was secured. He shoved her back and slammed the door. Someone got behind the wheel, and a moment later, the vehicle was underway.

She lay back and stretched out, willing the pain away so she could think.

Earlier, when they had pulled up to the clearing and gotten close to the four waiting men, Sarah had noticed all their untucked shirts had small rips by the bottom.

The same rip Jack Tate had on his shirt.

Chapter 16

Sam had waited long enough. He had tried calling Dolan's house again and got no answer. He then tried Dolan's cell without success.

That was half an hour ago. He tried the house phone one more time as he turned onto Dolan's street. Still nothing.

His tires squealed as he stopped in front of Dolan's house. At the front door, it sat ajar, lights on inside.

"Dolan?" Sam called. "You in there?"

He received no response. He didn't need a warrant to enter the house. Dolan was a friend. He pushed the door aside and stepped in. Everything looked as it should. He searched each floor quickly. With no sign of Dolan, he left through the front door, secured it, and ran back to his car.

It took him thirty minutes to get to the area on the highway where the two cops had been shot. A temporary tent had been erected to shield the incident from the public driving by. The two-lane highway was reduced to one as officers rerouted traffic around the site.

He showed his ID and pulled to the side, angling his car away from the setting sun. In the shade, he noticed the area was populated with people in FBI jackets.

How did the FBI get involved so fast?

Sam walked over to one of the few officers he recognized.

"Parkman, what're you doing here?"

"I could ask you the same thing. Don't they have you put away in the evidence locker?"

"And they have you at a desk, which begs the question again. What are you doing all the way out here? Are you working with the FBI?"

"I was the officer involved with the shooting this morning at Dolan's house, and I have a unique history with Sarah Roberts. Special Agent Jill Hanover asked for my assistance on this case, and the request was granted."

"Assistance on what case? Since when does the FBI get directly involved in a police shooting this fast?"

"Since today," a woman interjected.

He heard Hanover's familiar voice.

"Good to see everybody could join the party. What are you doing here, Johnson?"

"I just came from Dolan's house. We were supposed to meet there, but he wasn't home. I thought maybe he would be out here, you know, trying to conjure something up to help you."

"Is Dolan in trouble?" Hanover asked.

Sam shrugged and glanced at Parkman. "Who knows?" He looked at Hanover and decided to tell her what he saw at Dolan's. "His front door was ajar. There was no sign of a break-in, but I couldn't locate him."

Hanover turned away and spoke into her radio, telling an agent to go to Dolan's house.

Good, Sam thought, *that was the right move.*

She spun back to Sam. "I think we have all the help we need here."

An obvious dismissal.

"And I think I'm coming down with déjà vu. This reminds me of four years ago. Sarah kidnapped, I'm looking for her, and you step in to take over the case."

"Correct me if I'm wrong, but weren't you ordered to stay out of it or be charged with obstruction of justice? Yet you didn't, and you got shot for your efforts? Do us all a favor, Johnson, and go home. We got this." Hanover spun on her heels and walked away.

"I don't think she likes you," Parkman whispered.

"She has never liked me, but that doesn't matter. These are my friends. What can you tell me, Parkman?"

"Not much. The investigation is just getting started."

"Just tell me what you already know." Sam guided him to the side so they could talk privately.

"All I know so far is much of what you probably know. There's the dead guy in Tate's house and the guy I shot at Dolan's. Their names haven't popped up yet. I was back at the station filling out paperwork when I heard about this. Half an hour later, I got the call that the FBI had requested my presence. So here I am."

Sam gripped Parkman's arm and pulled him even farther from the makeshift tents.

"I can see it in your face. What else is going on?"

Parkman stared off into space for a moment. Sam followed his gaze and saw Hanover talking to two other FBI agents.

Parkman turned back. "They found handwritten notes on the ground."

"What kind of notes? What did they say?"

"I didn't get a chance to memorize it, but I know there was some personal stuff about one of the cops who was killed here. Stuff about his wife and how dangerous this job could be. It looks like it was Sarah who wrote it. That's why I was called in."

"What else?"

"Sam, Sarah didn't do what they think. They don't know her like we do."

"Parkman, tell me what else you know."

"The note said the officers would die. The FBI is taking that as a threat. It's in Sarah's handwriting. They've dusted the gun for prints. It appears to be Sarah's fingerprints on the gun that shot the guy in the black jacket. The way the FBI sees this is she shot the perp, and then her gun was empty. The gun that shot the officers was still in the perp's hand when we arrived. So either the perp shot the cops, or Sarah did because she was out of ammo, and then she placed the gun in his hand. Whichever way this goes down, it looks bad for Sarah."

"You and I both know that Sarah's always clean."

"Tell that to the FBI. They're the ones holding a threatening note written by Sarah."

"What would make them automatically assume Sarah would kill two cops?" Sam asked. "Even Hanover knows that wouldn't happen unless the cops were dirty and trying to kill Sarah."

"Sarah threatened two cops on paper, and then they were

shot. How do *you* think this looks? Also, everyone knows how much she hates cops. She hates us so much that she almost got herself killed four years ago instead of coming to us for help."

Sam shook his head, frustrated. "This is crazy, and it will only prove to Sarah that she can't trust us even more. You know as well as I do that every cop is trigger-happy when they're hunting a cop killer. I'd implore you to get that moniker off Sarah's back."

"I've tried to reason with them, but there's nothing I can do. I'm just the hired help. Special Agent Hanover is in charge. I'm just along for the ride, although I think it's because they know I'm the only cop Sarah might talk to. I think they had my phone records pulled or something."

"Phone records? What are you talking about?"

Parkman stepped back to let an officer walk by. When he was out of earshot, he turned back to Sam. "Sarah called me this afternoon. She said her parents had been kidnapped and she was being followed."

Sam raised his eyebrows and crossed his arms. "Her parents? What the hell is this? I'd bet ten to one that it's all connected to what happened four years ago. Otherwise, we've got an organized militia of some kind surgically taking out Sarah and everyone she's connected to, which sounds preposterous."

"I just can't figure out how Jack Tate is involved. I thought everyone was either killed or jailed four years ago."

Sam dropped his head, then looked up at Parkman, his eyes imploring. "You'll call me if something comes up? You know how I feel about these people."

"As soon as I can, I'll call," Parkman said and started

back toward Hanover.

Sam ran for his car, got in, and drove off, but not before he saw Hanover and two other FBI agents watching him leave.

Chapter 17

Sarah woke to a screaming bladder and a headache that shouted louder. The vehicle she was in slowed down. That must have been what woke her.

Did I black out, or was I sleeping?

She adjusted into a better position. Everything ached. Her shoulders, scalp, and most of all, her cheeks. She tried to smile, but it hurt too much.

These people were insane. Killing cops in broad daylight was crazy. Her life wasn't worth much to them, but she was sure she'd find out soon enough why they were keeping her alive. She also had to find out why everyone's shirts were torn at the base like Jack's. Could he be involved with them somehow?

Probably Jack led them into the trap, starting at Dolan's and ending at the highway kidnapping.

The SUV stopped, and the engine died. The driver got out and shut the door. With the blindfold on, she couldn't tell if the sun had gone down yet. Even though her hands were cuffed in the front, she didn't attempt to remove the blindfold. That would be asking for another beating.

As it turned out, it didn't matter because as the backdoor of the SUV opened, her blindfold was ripped away. She squinted, but her eyes adjusted quickly as it was already dark.

"Come on, get out."

The man standing at the back gate of the SUV was different from the one who had roughed her up earlier.

It was difficult with her hands cuffed, but she managed to get to the open door and dangle her legs out before she hopped off. Her new escort gripped her above the elbow and guided her away from the vehicle.

"Where are you taking me?" she asked.

He didn't respond.

"Where are the people I came with? Is Esmerelda here?"

She scanned the area. Small sheds, or huts, were lined in a row up ahead. They almost looked like the kind used on a lake when ice fishing. There were at least ten in a row. Some of them were secured with padlocks and chains wrapped around the door. The other ones had their doors sitting wide open. The bottoms of the sheds were sitting on concrete blocks.

"Is this the jail you plan on keeping me in?"

He pushed her toward one of the open sheds. Before being locked away, she tried to take in as much of the area as possible, but there wasn't much to see except a line of trees and darkness. Lights had been rigged up to shine directly on the door of each shed.

She looked down. "Why does everyone have a rip in their shirt?" she asked.

He stepped closer and gestured for Sarah to enter the hut.

She used the concrete block someone had placed on the ground as a step and entered the gloom of the dank-smelling room. The door shut behind her. She heard the lock snapping into place and the chains being slid across the door to secure her inside.

"Where's the bathroom?" she yelled through the door.

A moment later, his footsteps moved away from her shed.

It didn't take long to feel her way around the small hut. It was a square room with some kind of linoleum flooring. She found a small, raised platform in one corner. It was roughly the size of a small school chair, and it had a hole in it. Without feeling into the hole, she assumed it was the toilet from the subtle smell of an outhouse that emanated from it.

She eased her pants down and hovered over the hole. When she was finished, she felt around for toilet paper but came up empty-handed. After pulling up her pants, she continued her search of the tiny building.

The small hole was the only opening in the room besides the padlocked door.

She sat down in one of the corners and wondered why she still did this automatic writing stuff. It had been almost five years since she'd been listening to Vivian's messages. Was she cut out for it? Could she handle it? Would she respond to the vague family messages in the future? Life and death seemed so far apart when walking a downtown street with people milling around. But it was a line that was always close. One misstep, one miscalculation, and the end would come.

Sarah lowered her head into her arms and wept. She hadn't realized how tired she'd become. She felt the weight of exhaustion.

Why wouldn't Vivian help now? Why weren't the messages more specific whenever they had to do with family? Unless Vivian would tell her, Sarah feared she might never know.

Noises from outside came and went. A vehicle passed. She heard the gravel under someone's boots as they walked by.

Then Esmerelda shouted out in the distance.

Sarah jumped up in the dark. Her body resisted. She felt heavy with sleep.

Then Esmerelda's voice again. "Are you okay?"

"We're fine." It was her father's voice. She had barely been able to hear it.

They brought everyone here. But why?

"Mom! Dad! Can you hear me?" Sarah shouted.

She received no answer.

"Esmerelda!" she tried again.

Nothing. A soft rustle from behind her shed sounded like leaves on the trees moving as a wind picked up.

This posed new problems. Even if she could figure a way out of this building, they had all the people she loved trapped here. She couldn't just leave them behind.

She could get out and come back with help, but there were many problems with that. She had no idea where this compound was located. For all she knew, they could be a hundred miles from civilization. Even if she managed to escape, she would have to bring help back before they found out she was gone. She couldn't live with it if they hurt or killed anyone as punishment for her escaping.

She eased back down to the floor. Her fingers found a

few strands of hair on her forearm. New strands had grown in over the past few years. She rolled them between her fingers and tugged softly. The old feeling of pleasure wasn't there. The need, the desire to pull, was gone. She let the hair go and rested flat out on the linoleum floor.

Sleep took her in seconds.

Chapter 18

Sam Johnson flipped through the TV stations without watching any channels. He usually didn't mind a Saturday morning with nothing to do but not today. He was fidgety, tapping his foot and drumming his fingers.

For dozens of years, his response to being busy at work was to spend more time on the case he was working on. Ever since he transferred to the evidence room four years ago, he had adjusted well. He golfed, joined a chess club, and felt he was practically retired.

But now Sarah was in trouble again, along with many other people. It wasn't *just* Sarah this time. That's why he wanted in on this, even though his gut said to stay away.

He also knew it wasn't her fault. It couldn't be.

He flipped to the news channel as his phone rang.

He picked it up before the first ring stopped.

"Yeah?"

"Sam, it's Parkman."

"You got anything?"

"There is something."

"What?" Sam asked as he sat up on his couch.

"Keep this to yourself. I'm not supposed to involve you. The FBI wants this kept close to them because of how many kidnappings have happened in the last twenty-four hours."

"Of course. Just tell me what you got."

"Jack Tate used to be a cop twenty years ago."

"I knew that. Is there something new?"

"I pulled his file. He was under suspicion a couple of times for conduct unbecoming but never charged with anything."

Sam turned the TV off. He got up and headed for the bedroom to get dressed. He needed to do something, or he'd go crazy sitting around the house. "Go on."

"Jack Tate was following a lead the night he got shot. He was after a man named Armond Stuart. You'll remember Alex, Dolan's assistant?"

"I remember him quite well. What about it?"

"Armond is Alex's father."

"What? Jack was after Alex's father twenty years ago?"

"Here's the juicy part. I can't find anything on a guy named Armond Stuart. The guy doesn't exist. It's just a name. No social security number, no address, no nothing. The only thing I can come up with is he's really good at changing his identity."

Sam stopped in the doorway to his bedroom. "There's nothing? Are you sure?"

"Absolutely."

"Then how did Jack come up with the name during his investigation? He must've gotten it from somewhere."

"No one knows."

"How is that possible? He must've had a good enough source to write it in his reports," Sam said as he made it to his closet and started rifling through his dress shirts. He paused as an odd thought struck him. "Unless Jack made it up, or Jack Tate is Armond himself."

"No one will ever know. After he took a bullet to the head, he got amnesia. He retired on disability after recovering in the hospital. Been living like a recluse ever since. His neighbors claim they rarely see him."

"Okay, I'm not saying there's anything wrong with this Jack Tate guy, but my radar is pinging. Questions are going to have to be answered. After Jack was shot all those years ago, what happened to the investigative work he had done up until then? Didn't anybody else take over his cases?"

"I'm still looking into that, among other things. It looks like a lot is missing."

Sam selected a blue-collared shirt and tugged it one-handed off the hanger. "I'm heading out. Can we meet up later?"

"Sure."

"Okay, Parkman, I'll call you." Sam hung up.

He got changed and left the house. He knew Officer Winnfield was the cop who talked to Jack Tate the other night.

Maybe there was something he could say that would shed light on this.

Chapter 19

THE DOOR TO HER tiny prison opened, causing Sarah to squint into the bright morning sun. It was the same guy who had hit her yesterday.

"Get up," he said.

She got to her knees and then used the wall for support to stand. She was stiff from a night on the hard floor. Her face still ached from the punch.

The man grabbed her arm and forcefully pulled her from the little room. Pain flared in her wrists where the cuffs were starting to chafe.

She had to cover her eyes as the morning sun shone directly on her face.

They walked down a path cut between the small sheds. Most of them had their doors sitting open, empty.

As her eyes focused better, she looked around. Trees surrounded the compound. Besides the path they were on that led between the sheds, she couldn't see past the line of trees.

One man escorting her was a risk which meant security

had to be good. They had no fear of her trying to escape.

By the time they got to the end of the sheds, she had counted at least twenty, ten on each side. Would they be harboring that many victims at any given time? Who *were* these people that they could kidnap at random and kill cops?

A larger building was up ahead, like a small airplane hangar with a barn on the side. So far, she could not see any fences or gates. What were these people thinking? If she broke out of her shed, she could just run into the trees and be gone.

Maybe it wasn't as easy as it looked. She figured they must have some kind of security in the trees, like cameras or other men just waiting for captives to break out. Or maybe that was just it—secure the prisoner so well that you do not need added security. Lock them up tight and be done with it. On the outside, this place would look like a summer camp.

They made it to the entrance of the barn-shaped building beside the hangar. The brute let go of her arm and stepped back.

The main door opened, and an odd-looking man wearing black-rimmed glasses stepped out.

"Come in, Sarah," he said with a gesture.

"What's going on? What is this place?"

Something clicked behind her. She turned to look. The man had a gun, cocked, and aimed at her.

"I want to be the one who kills you," he whispered. "Run, try to escape, please, just do it when I'm watching. I need to be the one."

"Blake, stand down. Sarah, come, enter this building."

Sarah remembered the guy's face. He was the one she had pistol-whipped in front of Jack Tate's house. "What happened to your face?" she asked. "You've got a nasty red mark on the side."

He shoved his weapon toward her until she was looking down the barrel. "Ask me that again, little bitch, ask me again," he said, his teeth clenched.

"You sound like you enjoy being tough," Sarah said as the tip of the gun pushed into her nose. "I'll remember that, *and* I'll make sure you're one of the first ones *I* kill when this is over."

She backed away and moved toward the building even though her legs were shaking. Men like that were the reason she did what she did. Because men like that shouldn't and couldn't exist in a civil society where mothers and their children also existed.

At the door, she turned back. Blake had lowered his weapon. He was easing it back into a shoulder holster under his black jacket.

"Weren't you loved as a child?" Sarah asked, then turned and entered the building.

Inside, the lights had been dimmed. The place was crowded with tables and desks. It looked like a planning station for a wartime drill. Something she'd seen in a movie.

Crazy Glasses guided her to a corridor that led away from the main room. After twenty paces down the darkened hall, he opened a door and told her to go in and wait.

A table and chair sat in the middle of the room. On it was a pad of paper and a pen.

Glasses shut the door behind her. She walked around the room looking for cameras or peepholes. The room appeared to be sealed off. She had only two minutes alone before the door opened. Blake and two other men filed in. Sarah backed up to the corner.

"Sit," one of the men ordered.

"I'd rather stand," Sarah replied. If there was anything she had learned over the years, it was to establish some kind of control even when none could be had.

The man closest to her pulled something from under his jacket and swung hard. Before it hit her, Sarah recognized it was a strap of some kind. In the second it registered mentally, the strap lashed across her left shoulder and collar bone. Intense pain crippled her ability to stand.

She fell to her knees and held her shoulder as best she could with cuffed wrists. She used her feet to push herself away from the man who still wielded the strap.

"Damn!" she shouted. "That fuckin' hurts. Get away from me." Her efforts to avoid the man came to a halt at the wall.

He swung the strap back and forth and then collected it into a ball. "Get up and sit in the chair, or I will whip you to a bloody pulp."

He spoke with a British accent.

She used her right hand and arm to balance herself and got to her feet. Sweat beaded up on her forehead. The pain made her woozy. When she eased the chair out to sit, she saw each man in the room sported a rip in their shirt.

She hunched her back when she sat and used her right hand to reach gingerly inside her shirt and feel the wound. Blood had formed on the surface of the skin. Her hand came away crimson.

What the hell is on that whip? Studs?

"Tell us what you do."

"What I do? What are you talking about?"

The man unfolded the whip and stepped closer.

"Okay, okay, what I do." She glanced back at the table with the pen and paper and guessed they already had the answer to what they were asking. "Are you talking about automatic writing? I'm assuming that's what you're talking about, right?"

The man with the whip nodded. He stepped closer, produced a key, and with deft hands, undid her cuffs.

Sarah gently massaged the feeling back into her wrists.

"I have no control over it," she said, keeping an eye on the man with the strap. "It happens when it happens. I blackout anywhere from a few seconds to a full minute. While in the blackout, I have no conscious idea what's happening. For me, it's lost time. When I came to, there was a note of some kind with a message. I follow the instructions. That's it."

No one responded. The three men stood in a semi-circle, watching her.

"What?" she asked. "Is there anything else?"

The man who had removed her cuffs said, "How come you can save all those people from a burning building, but you can't save yourself?"

"I have no idea." They had researched her in detail. Strap Man stepped closer.

"What?" Sarah asked. "I really have no idea."

"You are going to explain things until we are content with your answer. You will know we are content when we ask another question. Otherwise, there will be consequences."

She leaned her body against the table. The pain ebbed. It felt like she'd been burned. She took her eyes off them and lowered her head. "Each message is different. Some come with specific details, while others don't. The ones with details are easier for me to manage. Usually, messages that involve something personal to me are the ones that aren't specific. It would've been great to get one that told me to avoid you guys, but, alas, that didn't happen."

She feared her attitude would inspire them to cause her more harm, but no one moved.

"Give us an example of a specific message."

She looked him in the eye, knowing where this was going and not liking it. These were the kind of men who kill cops. There was no way she or anyone else would leave here alive. The only thing she had left was time.

"I once received a message that said, '*Sit directly in the middle, under the St. Elizabeth Bridge. 10:18 a.m. Bring hammer.*' I did exactly as it said to do."

"And what happened?"

"At 10:18 a.m., there was an accident on the bridge above. A car broke through the guardrail and fell to the river below. It landed upside down. The car was damaged enough that I couldn't get in to pull the driver out. The river water seeped in fast. The female driver would've drowned if I hadn't had the hammer. She was upside down, suspended by her seatbelt. I used the hammer to break the glass, rolled into the back, and lifted her head just in time. Firefighters took over from there." She looked at each man. "Is that what this is all about?"

"As I recall, you saved a news anchorwoman that day. Tell us why you do it."

Sarah sat up straighter and placed her hands on her thighs. "I do it because I have to."

"What do you mean *you have to*?"

"When the blackouts began, I didn't respond to the first few messages. People got hurt. A girl down the street from where I used to live got beat up pretty badly. If I don't act on the messages I receive, people die. I can't have that on my conscience. I've been doing it so long that I trust I'll get out of it unscathed. Like this scenario. I'll walk away from this, and you three will either be in jail or dead. My preference is dead."

Strap Man moved forward. Question Man waved him off.

"Is this something you were told in your messages?"

Should she lie? Would they be able to tell? Her conscience got the better of her.

"No. It's something I know. I've been in worse situations and walked away. There's a reason you haven't killed the other people you have here or me."

Question Man stepped around behind her.

"Who do you think we have here?"

"Esmerelda, Jack Tate, my parents."

"So you don't know who else?"

Sarah turned around to look at him.

"It's okay," he said. "You don't have to answer that last question. In about five minutes, it won't matter what you know."

Blake pulled out a revolver.

Question Man continued, "There's one bullet in that gun. We need you to do your thing with that piece of paper and start writing. Every time you blackout and write a prophecy, we move the clock back. If you write nothing, every sixty seconds, my colleague here will point the gun at your head and pull the trigger. The most amount of time you have left to live is five minutes. The least amount, one minute."

She instantly felt sick. She wanted to get up and smash his face into the wall but knew there was no way she could get past all of them.

"Are we clear? The clock starts now."

"Wait … what, what are you—"

"Sarah, you don't have time to talk." He pointed at the paper on the table. "You need to write something, or you will die."

This couldn't be real. "That's not how it works!"

"Goodbye, Sarah," Question Man said as he headed for the door.

"It's involuntary! I pass out. I have no control over it. You have to listen to me."

He stopped at the door, his hand on the knob. "Well, then, you had better pass out. Let's see which one of us gets out of here alive after all, eh, Sarah?" He looked at his watch. "Thirty seconds until the first game of Russian Roulette."

He stepped out, followed by the other man. Only Blake and his weapon stayed behind.

"You have to listen to me," she said. "Put the *fucking* gun away. What are you doing this for? It's ridiculous."

Blake brought the tip of the weapon to her temple and stared at his watch.

"Look, give me time. I always write something eventually." Her heart raced. Something in her soul shouted *no, it'll be okay*.

At the one-minute mark, she opened her mouth to protest.

He pulled the trigger.

Chapter 20

SAM HAD RARELY WORKED a case with so few clues. Actually, he had nothing to go on. He wasn't supposed to be trying to track anything down, but he couldn't stay home.

Officer Winnfield was back on duty this morning. Sam knew exactly where to find him.

Sam parked in his usual spot and walked straight to the second floor, where he found Winnfield at his desk, sipping coffee.

"Winnfield, you got a sec?"

Officer Winnfield set his coffee down and leaned back in his chair. "Sure, Johnson, what do you need?"

"I want to talk to you about Jack Tate."

Winnfield looked around at the desks nearest to his. "I can't talk about that."

Sam frowned. "Why not? What's the problem?"

"The FBI took it over," Winnfield said. "Listen, Sam, let's go across the street and grab a coffee. What do you say?"

Ten minutes later, they were seated opposite each other, Sam having a normal coffee with just cream and Winnfield having a latte.

"What's going on?" Sam asked. "Why the covert conversation?"

Winnfield looked around the coffee shop like they were being watched. "There's so much going on I don't even know where to start."

"Come on, Winnfield, stop being so cryptic. Just tell me what's up."

"I've been pushing Parkman for information because I was pissed the FBI walked in and took me off the case. Then they let Jack Tate walk. I mean, why is Jack so important? I think the FBI will have to answer that question because as soon as Jack is set free, some guy dies in the front foyer of Jack's house. The dead guy has a bullet in his knee that looks like it came from Sarah Roberts's gun and a knife in the thigh that came from Jack's kitchen."

"I know all this. I talked to Parkman, too."

"Did you know that the dead guy also had a rip in his shirt, just like Jack's and the dead girl discovered in the woods by Jack's house?"

Sam wasn't sure he heard him right. "How could that be?" He glanced up and watched as three teenagers entered the coffee shop. It gave him time to ponder his next sentence. "Could Jack Tate be killing people and marking them with a ripped shirt?"

Winnfield shook his head. "I don't think so. I think this is something bigger. Bigger than Jim Jones or that David guy in Waco."

"What makes you say that?"

Winnfield leaned in close and lowered his voice. "I can't say much because I don't know all of it, but they got the retreating vehicle's license plate from a witness on the highway where our two colleagues were murdered. When they ran the plates, according to Parkman, they belonged to a college professor on the other side of the city. A couple of uniforms went over to look into it. Apparently, the professor's plates were lifted off his vehicle two nights ago. But get this, so were ten other license plates in the same neighborhood. So whoever these guys are, it looks like they have at least ten vehicles and change plates routinely. I haven't seen this kind of activity in all my time as a police officer."

Winnfield leaned in so close Sam could smell the latte on his breath.

"You know, a lot of people have gone missing since last night," Sam said as he sipped his coffee. "Has anything come in on the dead girl by Jack's place?"

Winnfield shook his head. "Her fingerprints were burned off and her teeth removed. There's evidence of some kind of sexual torture, but nothing conclusive until the autopsy report returns in a few days, which I won't get access to. They've estimated her age to be around sixteen. I'm starting to feel that this has something to do with human trafficking."

A couple of more teenagers entered the coffee shop. Their loud, boisterous conversation caught Sam's attention. He watched them for a moment and then looked back at Winnfield, who was already talking.

"What was that?" Sam asked. "Missed some of it."

"I was just saying that I've been ordered to finish my reports and then hand them over to the FBI and to not talk about this case with anyone. I'm supposed to let it go."

It was a big case for him to land. To have it ripped out from under him by the Feds lost him the collar. Sam remembered that about Winnfield, how he always looked for something that could make him stand out and get noticed.

"Winnfield, I gotta run," Sam said. "Thanks for the coffee." Sam got up to leave, pushing his chair in.

"Hey, Sam, you'll let me know if you find anything, right?"

"Of course, Winnfield. Of course."

Sam patted his shoulder as he walked by him on the way to the door. He took one last look at the teenagers and knew everyone had to look out for themselves in today's society. He felt sorry for their youth. There really wasn't any protection for the public.

The police always got there too late.

Chapter 21

A WETNESS OOZED THROUGH Sarah's pants. Her bladder had released, surrendering its warmth.

Blake lowered the gun and looked at his watch. In her panic, her mind blanked.

They're actually going to kill me.

"Do you have a dog?" she asked.

He didn't look away from his watch.

"How about a cat? Any kind of pet? You were a kid once. Didn't you have hopes and dreams? Is this what you wanted to be when you grew up?"

Still no response. The guy was as disciplined as a machine. She would be dead in minutes, and he wouldn't even acknowledge her existence.

A tear leaped to her eye.

Shit. Why do I cry at moments like these?

"Do you feel anything like the rest of us?" Sarah asked. "Are you human?" She lowered her head. "You know, if you had a pet, a companion, maybe your heart would heal. Maybe you could join the human race again."

Then she realized what she had to do.

She turned away from Blake and grabbed the pen. Mentally, she tried to figure out how much time she had left before he would shoot again. She figured she had at least twenty seconds.

There was no way she could reason with these people. She had to beat them another way.

She held the pen tight, rocking back and forth in the chair to the imagined rhythm of seconds on a clock. After a count of twenty, Blake had raised the gun to aim it at her.

With only seconds left, she rolled her eyes back as far as she could and slumped into the chair. Her hand worked the paper furiously. She wrote whatever came to mind. After a few moments, she dropped the pen and slipped out of the chair.

Her urine from earlier was cold on her butt when she hit the floor. She bumped her elbow but kept the groan buried.

She was sure at least ten seconds had passed. She hadn't heard the click of the gun.

Blake picked up the paper. She waited while he read it, holding her breath.

She had done what they'd asked for. She had blacked out and written down a prophecy. What would come next?

She moved on the floor and moaned. Then, with her insides rolling around like she might vomit, Sarah lifted her head. Blake stood by the door, the paper in his hand. His gun had been put back into its holster.

She edged out from under the table, confident that her ruse might have worked. At least the gun was gone, so she'd made some progress.

Her pants were heavier. She wanted to cry again.

Blake stood rigid as he stared at her.

She made it up into the chair and sat, trying to look defeated. The smell of urine bothered her nose. She was sure she would throw up if the door wasn't opened in the next few minutes. A flare of anger rose in her because she hated being so weak, feminine, and soft. There were times to be feminine and revel in it, and there were times to be tough. This was one of those times when she needed to be tough.

Blake moved fast. He had pulled his gun out again, but this time he held it backward, the butt of the handle facing her.

"Aren't we done here?" she asked.

"You have a debt to pay," he said.

"What debt?"

"I owe you for the pistol-whipping at Jack's place," Blake said.

He swung his arm back and stepped in. His speed was incredible. Before she could respond, the handle of the gun struck her on the side of the face so hard she rocked violently into the table, then bounced off it to the floor.

As she slithered like warm butter to the ground, her last thought was, *can I die from such a blow?*

Chapter 22

THE PAIN THROBBED IN her ear. It was like she could hear the ache. Sarah gingerly touched her face where it was swollen and tender.

Why do I do this shit to myself again and again?

It's not like she got paid for it. All she ever got was trouble from the cops and the criminals. At one point, she thought having the ability to foresee events and then change them to help people would be good. She had saved lives, but this gift also put her life in peril all too often. Maybe, just maybe, if she got out of this alive, she would consider giving it up. Let people kill themselves and maim each other with all their stupidity. Who was Sarah Roberts to stand in their way?

She rolled to her side. The ache in her face made her wonder if her cheek was broken. Maybe the blow had cracked the orbital bone around her eye. She felt the floor in the darkness and confirmed she was back in her little prison.

The beatings had to stop. If something wasn't done soon, Sarah would die in this compound, along with everyone else they had imprisoned here.

She moved to the wall, felt her way to the door, and ran her hands across its surface, looking for weaknesses. It was rock solid. On bended knee, she felt the edge of the linoleum and traced it for a few feet. It was bonded to the wall in a solid grip.

Without tools of some kind, there was no way out.

Discouraged, she shuffled over to the hole with the raised seat. A faint urine smell wafted up. It mixed well with the subtle scent still coming from her wet pants. Her fingers paused on the clasp as she went to undo her pants.

The hole.

Where did it lead? How far down did it go? If she got under the shed, could she find a section of the wall where it would be weak enough to push through?

It gave her hope.

She measured the hole as best she could. It was about the circumference of a basketball. Her shoulders wouldn't get through.

She braced herself, grabbed the edge of the hole, and pulled upward to break a piece off. Nothing moved. She pulled again, as hard as she could. Still nothing. There wasn't even a creaking to signal strain on the wood.

How the hell was she going to budge it?

It seemed fruitless to continue trying to pull pieces apart. She couldn't jump on the edge. It was too dark to see what she was doing. If anyone were outside, they would hear the stomping.

What now?

She shuffled close to the hole's edge, reached through, and touched the ground below. Normally, this act would make her pull her hand back and grimace. But right now, grimacing only flared her headache, and she couldn't pull her hand back. She had to find a way out of there.

Within seconds she found what she was looking for. Rocks and small pebbles were mixed with the random dirt under the shed. She located the biggest rock she could find, which was about the size of a small baseball. She felt its edges for any that might be sharp.

From the time she woke up until now, she had heard nothing from outside. No light emanated from under the shed's door. For what she had in mind to work, it would be better if it was early morning.

Sarah lowered her pants and urinated on the edge of the hole, making sure to soak the wood surrounding the area she was going to focus on.

When she was finished, she did her pants back up and waited for the urine to work its way in.

She put her ear against the shed wall to listen for anyone who might be close but heard nothing.

She slid across the linoleum floor and felt around the edge of the hole. It was still wet. There would be no way to mask the banging. This was her only chance. If it didn't work, she would be out of options.

She held the rock aloft in her right hand and said a quick prayer. Then she brought it crashing down on the wooden edge of the hole. Again and again, she smashed the rock into the wood. By the third hit, anger fueled violence in her. She felt the madness of the situation overwhelm her. She grunted in frustration with each downward stroke. She grunted at the unfairness of it all and the sheer viciousness of these people.

The wood finally cracked under the blows. She stopped

and dropped the rock, panting.

Her fingers found the split wood. She had made a small crack in the edge. Elated, she picked the rock up and dedicated her violence to the damaged area.

Another crack resounded throughout the shed. She stopped and listened if anyone approached from the outside. It was hard to hear anything because of the pounding in her ears.

She stood over the hole, grabbed the split rim with both hands, and yanked. It cracked again and broke away. She lost her balance and fell back a bit. When she examined her work, she realized it would be big enough for her shoulders.

Someone shouted outside, and a vehicle's engine revved.

They had been alerted by her noise.

She dropped her head down into the hole first. The stench filled her nostrils—rotting earth mixed with human excrement embedded in the dirt long ago. She lifted her head back out and took a deep breath of the cleaner air.

They were close. At any second, her door would burst open. She had no idea what she was going to do. How would dropping into the hole help her now? This might have actually been really stupid, but it was all she could think to do at the time.

She took one more deep breath and dropped her head into the hole. Her shoulders eased into the opening and filled it. With a slight nudge, they popped through. She wedged her right hand ahead and felt her way to the ground, supporting her weight on her forearm and elbow.

Someone was at the shed's door behind her. The locks clicked against the chains that secured the tiny prison.

Time had run out.

With her left arm pulled through, she moved into the wet and cool earth under the shed. The linoleum floor of her shed was about two feet above the dirt floor. It was just enough room for her to crawl along on her arms.

The chains that secured her door were being ripped out of their loops. The door would open any second.

She crawled away from the gaping hole, pulling her legs in after her.

Her feet touched the earth under the piss hole and dug in to help thrust her away from the opening.

Meager light cast down the hole as the door to her shed opened.

Multiple pairs of boots rushed in. Someone barked out commands.

She moved toward the edge of the space underneath the raised shed. A light shone past her. Someone had stuck their head in the hole with a flashlight, and then it was gone.

"I can't breathe in there," a man yelled. "She pissed all over the fucking hole. My hand has urine on it."

"Take another look and confirm whether she is down there."

Sarah crawled as far as she could and hit the secured wall. She could go no farther. As soon as the flashlight came through the hole again, they would find her trapped like a mouse in a corner.

What the hell do I do now?

She grabbed the cool, wet dirt and smeared it on her face. She fought the urge to throw up and swallowed the bile that crept along her throat.

"Okay, give me a sec," the man above said. "Let me catch a good breath first."

She was close enough to hear the man with the flashlight breathing in and out. That gave her another precious second to cover herself with more dirt. As she massaged it, she bumped her wounded cheek and almost screamed out in pain.

Light filled the area where she had entered. The flashlight holder dropped his head in and scoured around in a circle. The flashlight passed by her but didn't stop. She had buried her face and hands in the ground directly in front of her just in time.

The flashlight holder shuffled back out of the hole. He took large gulps of air.

"Well?" someone else asked.

"She's not … she's not down there. She's gone."

Sarah lifted her head out of the dirt and breathed in a quiet and controlled manner. She heard footsteps above her and a few curse words muffled by the floor.

"Find her! She couldn't have gotten far. I want the entire area scoured. Shoot on sight. We cannot let this one get away. That's an order. Do you all hear me? Shoot her on sight."

"Sir, yes, sir!"

Sarah didn't move for a few minutes. The intensity of the smell eased as she got used to it.

In a spinning motion, Sarah rolled close to the broken hole in the shed's floor. A soft light illuminated the room above her. They hadn't closed the main door.

That's right, she thought. *Leave it open.*

She raised her head out of the hole and risked a peek into the room. It was empty.

With nothing left but luck, she gripped the more solid edge of the hole's rim and lifted herself out. Her running shoes made no sound as she stood on the linoleum. She crept up to the wall beside the open door.

She was about to peek out but stopped at the door frame. The sun had started to rise. It was getting brighter outside. She'd be visible to anyone watching the door.

A sudden urge to get away from the door struck her. These people wouldn't just run away and start looking for her throughout the complex. If they heard her banging around in the shed and seconds later she disappeared, they would assume she was close. Very close.

They didn't think she was inside, but they weren't stupid. Someone would be watching her shed.

A feeling like she was running out of time overcame her. She strode back across the floor and slipped effortlessly into the piss hole. Sprawled out on the dirt below, she could swear someone was at the door, looking in.

She froze and listened. *Was that the soft rustle of a jacket?*

Sarah rolled across the dirt, aiming for the corner again. When she got there, she dipped her face and hands toward the outer wall.

Someone walked across the floor above her.

Then the floor exploded as whoever was standing above fired multiple rounds into it. She turned to look and saw bullet holes forming above her, off to the side.

She almost screamed out in panic.

The gun changed direction. The holes started forming closer.

Sarah knew if she made a noise, she would certainly die down here. If she were recaptured, she would die. If the bullets hit her, she would die.

She pushed herself into the wall as far as she could.

When the first bullet hit her arm, she didn't cry out. She passed out.

Chapter 23

SAM JOHNSON PULLED INTO the roadside truck stop on the edge of town. He spied Parkman's sedan immediately and pulled in beside it.

Sunday morning, and the place looked packed. Rigs were lined up along the sides and the back of the building, indicating to Sam how full the restaurant would be.

He got out and walked to the front door. A couple held the door for him as he entered.

Parkman had found a table in the back corner. On the way there, his fellow officer saw him, dropped the menu he was looking at, and motioned for the waitress.

"Why meet way out here?" Sam asked.

"One sec," Parkman motioned as the waitress walked up.

After placing an order for a breakfast special and a coffee for Sam, the waitress left.

"First, have you learned anything new?" Parkman asked.

Sam shook his head. "Nothing. I talked to other officers, but everyone has been kept out of the loop."

Parkman nodded. "Even me."

"You? I thought the FBI took you on to help. You know more about Sarah Roberts than anybody except Sarah."

"They have what I know already. I was told they didn't need me anymore. I had to sign a confidentiality waiver."

The waitress walked up. They stopped talking as she set a coffee down in front of Sam.

When she walked away, Sam said, "Tell me everything."

"There's nothing to tell. After discussing Sarah at length, they let me go. I'm supposed to report back to my desk on Monday morning."

Sam clasped his hands together to avoid smacking the table. "You know, I'm getting pretty frustrated with this whole thing."

"Me too."

"How can so many people get kidnapped in the last twenty-four hours, and no one knows a thing? The only lead we can come up with is ripped shirts and license plates that are stolen from the same neighborhood."

Parkman's head shot up. "I just remembered. A sixteen-year-old girl went missing in Utah."

"What's that got to do with this?"

"She was seen here, downtown, two days ago, with three men, by a witness who knows the family in Utah. He had just figured he had a case of mistaken identity, but when he called the family, he discovered the girl was missing."

"People go missing all the time, Parkman. We both know that. Just not so many in one area."

He leaned in closer. "Yeah, but there's more."

Sam raised his eyebrows.

"The witness told Special Agent Jill Hanover that the

men wore ripped shirts. The rip was about two inches long and cut at an angle. After the witness confirmed with the family in Utah that the girl was missing, he called the police in this area. I heard about this an hour before Agent Hanover told me I would return to my desk on Monday."

"How would a potential witness see that kind of detail without being right up in front of these guys?" Sam asked.

"I'm getting the feeling this has something to do with human trafficking. A large organization identified by their ripped shirts—"

Sam's cell phone rang. He pulled it out and frowned. He raised a finger to gesture for Parkman to wait.

"Hello?"

"Sam Johnson?"

The voice was deep like the caller was trying to disguise it.

"This is Sam. Who am I talking to?"

"I'm calling to talk to you about an exchange."

Sam looked at Parkman. "What kind of exchange are we talking about?"

"Call it a two-for-one deal. I will give you two people in exchange for one."

"I'm going to need a little more than that."

"All you need to know for now are the names of the people involved in the trade."

"I'm listening," Sam said as he reached into his jacket to pull out a pad and pen.

"I will give you both of Sarah Roberts's parents, Amelia and her husband, Caleb. I'd actually be happy to get rid of Caleb. He has proven to be quite a problem."

Sam felt the color leave his face. This was the closest

anyone had gotten to this group in days. He had to go along. But who could they want in exchange? This was over his head. Yet the last thing he would like to do was give this to the assholes at the FBI.

"In exchange," the caller continued, "I want you."

He heard it said so quickly that he wasn't sure he heard it right.

"Excuse me? Who do you want?"

"I want you in exchange for the parents. Does this work for you? I will give you three seconds to give me a yes or a no."

The answer was spontaneous. He spoke before he could do a gut check.

"Yes."

"Good. I will call you back within the hour. Talk to no one about this. You're not stupid. You know how this works. If we see any problem, the parents die. And get rid of Parkman. We don't want him."

Chapter 24

With his coffee finished and an excuse to leave, Sam jumped in his car and started driving back into town.

How could whoever called know he was with Parkman? Had they tapped his phone? Were they tailing Parkman or both of them? The biggest question of all was, why him?

He had fought in the line of duty before, been shot and almost killed, but he never willingly walked into the bear's cave, knowing full well that he probably wouldn't walk out.

Could he even go through with it?

His hands shook on the steering wheel. What would happen if he didn't go through with this suicide mission? Could he live with it if Amelia and Caleb were found dead in a ditch?

Sarah's parents would die, and it would be on his head if he didn't go through with it. He said yes so readily because he knew he had no choice.

The police always get there too late.

He was duty-bound. *To protect and serve.* A nervous

laugh escaped his lips.

"To protect and serve," he said out loud. "That's funny."

He'd done that his whole adult life. His reward was the evidence room. He admitted part of that decision was his, but if he hadn't agreed, they would've put him there anyway, or worse.

Even though he almost died four years ago trying to save Sarah, he had disobeyed direct orders to stay clear. He'd been warned, by none other than Special Agent Jill Hanover, that he would be charged if he got involved.

Instead of being arrested in his hospital room, they offered him a job where he wouldn't get in anyone else's way.

Two days ago, he wouldn't even have contemplated this. Two days ago, he was considering what movies to rent for the weekend.

As much as life had become quiet, he had been getting itchy to do something more important.

Not only did he risk further trouble by showing up at the scene where two fellow officers were killed, but he might have risked his job once Hanover saw him asking Parkman questions.

Was there a connection with the FBI? Maybe the FBI had undercover operatives working inside the criminal network? Nothing about this case made sense to Johnson. By agreeing to do the exchange, he hoped he had it in him to go through with it. His only prayer was that the FBI had infiltrated this group and wanted to bring them down.

He drove fast and made it home forty-five minutes after he received the call. He rushed in and opened his gun cabinet. His Drop Point knife sat right where it was supposed to be.

Sam lifted it out and unsheathed the blade. It was designed for big game hunting with a robust, curved blade of thick steel, allowing him to remove an animal's skin easily. He liked it so much because the steel blade protruded in a unique way to allow for easy slicing of a combatant if it ever came to that.

He strapped the knife to his inner thigh.

This was indeed a suicide mission.

Once the parents were safe and out of the perp's control, Sam meant to do as much damage as possible.

There was no way they'd let him have a gun. Someone would frisk him. But a knife might pass a lazy inspection if it was on the upper inside of his thigh.

At least, he hoped he was right.

His life depended on it.

The cell phone in his jacket rang. At the sound, his heart and stomach dropped.

"This is it," he said loudly and answered the phone.

"Are you ready?" the deep voice from earlier asked.

Chapter 25

Sarah fluttered her eyelids as she came to. Something stank badly. She forced air out of her nostrils and shook her head to clear it. Pain seemed to be everywhere, and when she shook her head, it flared in her face and arm.

"Ooohhh," she moaned.

Quiet, she reminded herself.

Too late. It was out. She could only hope no one was close enough to hear. She waited and listened, breathing in and out slowly, remaining quiet.

After a minute, she moved. Her muscles responded with protest. Parts of her were either stiff or injured.

It was pitch black under the shed. She couldn't see a glimmer of light anywhere. She tried to spin her body around while running through what had happened.

She had almost escaped and then thought better of running for it. She had hidden under the floor. They'd already checked there. The last place they'd think to look was back in her prison.

But someone had followed her back in. She was sure no one had seen her, only suspected she was there. They had shot the floor up. Bullets hit her.

She scoured her body for new injuries. Her left arm was cut badly, and a bloody wetness had formed on her leg. She used her right hand to inspect the leg and felt a small scab crusted over an area where a bullet might have just nicked her.

The ache in her left arm was the same thing but deeper. She could feel a gouge near the top of her triceps. She got hit with two bullets, but both only grazed her enough that they could clot on their own. Otherwise, she would have bled out in this shit hole and died.

She couldn't roll like before because of her left arm and leg wound. The last thing she wanted was to get any more of the filthy dirt into the open wounds, even though they'd crusted over.

As gently as she could, Sarah moved, using all of her right arm and some of her uninjured leg, and pushed toward where she thought the hole in the shed would be. In the absolute darkness, she misjudged by a couple of feet. The wood above her was littered with holes where bullets had searched for her.

A burning desire to get out from under the shed and into fresh air drove her to struggle against the pain and the smell. She could feel the dirt still encrusted in her hair and neck when she tried to cover herself with it in an attempt to hide.

Nowhere in the travel guide did it say I'd get shot and have fun crawling around in a shit hole that was literally *filled with shit.*

Her fingers caressed the edge of the broken hole. With

careful and quiet motions, she got herself up and sat on the edge, where she hesitated to catch her breath.

When was the last time she'd eaten? Breakfast with Jack at least twenty-four hours ago?

The loudest noise in this tiny jail was her stomach.

Sarah got up and walked to the open door. The darkness was broken by the scattered lights around some of the sheds. She couldn't see a single person anywhere.

With her good shoulder leaning on the door frame, she peeked around the door and scanned the entire area in front of the shed.

Earlier, when she had almost walked out, the sun had just been rising. Now, it felt like it was very early in the morning. That meant she had been under the floor for almost twenty-four hours. Did she have a head injury? A concussion?

A quick feel of her head determined there were no new injuries.

How did I lose a day?

She had two choices. Leave her makeshift jail and try to get as far from here as possible or wait under the floor for however long until rescue comes.

Why wait? What rescue?

Her experience with police procedures told her that there would be no rescue. She had to get out on her own. She always had to take care of herself.

With a careful step, Sarah walked out into the open.

She waited for a bullet to hit her or an alarm to sound, but nothing came as she retreated into the trees behind the line of tiny jails.

A sense of freedom moved through her, but also a sense of sadness because—though *she* might be getting away—

people close to her would still be held captive.

She rushed headlong into the foliage navigating with what little light the moon offered. At least her eyes had adjusted enough not to walk into a tree. Her leg wound throbbed noticeably, but it didn't stop her. She took deep breaths to rid her nostrils of the horrid smell of the shit hole, but it didn't work because she was still covered in dirt. She wondered if she would ever get rid of that disgusting smell even when she showered and changed.

In minutes she had left the lights of the compound behind. The trees opened up, becoming sparser as she walked into an open field. She couldn't see the other side of the field in the dark but could tell another line of trees was there.

To catch her breath, Sarah slowed and scanned the area. The only light in evidence was a minute ray filtering through the trees from where she had come.

For concealment, the group must have built the sheds hidden among the copse of trees near that main farm building they had taken her to for the interrogation. No one would see a thing unless they were looking from above.

With no plan but to get as far away from the compound as possible, Sarah continued walking through the open field.

The night air was cool and refreshing. She walked on, knowing that the thugs could, or would, hurt the people close to her as revenge for her escape.

At least half an hour passed before the sky brightened in the east.

Sarah had traversed hills and small thickets of brush but hadn't crossed a road.

Maybe she was walking parallel to a road. She turned to the right, which was still heading away from the compound, and continued.

As the edge of the sun crested the hillside, Sarah saw her first glimpse of civilization. A dirt road was roughly five hundred yards ahead. It led to a small white farmhouse. No lights were on, nor were there any cars in the driveway. It didn't look abandoned. As she drew closer, there was a large aboveground pool in the backyard beside the porch, but the water looked odd. Upon closer inspection, she discovered it wasn't the water but a green pool cover lying across the top.

She walked right up to the siding near the back corner of the house without interruption. When she placed an ear to the wall, she heard nothing. It didn't mean the house was empty, though. Cautiously, Sarah crept toward the backdoor. With a final look around the field behind the house, she opened the screen door and tried the inner door handle. It was locked. She eased the screen back into place.

She glanced into the living room window when she got around to the front of the house. The furniture looked new and expensive, like whoever owned this house had money. She prayed no one was home and that they wouldn't come home anytime soon so she could shower, borrow some of their clothes and contact the authorities.

She eased up the front steps, her aches and pains forgotten for the moment. The only things moving in the early morning sun were the birds that seemed extra happy this morning, judging by their chirping.

She tried the front door, only to find it locked, too.

She looked horrible, covered in dirt, bloody and bruised, but she really had no choice. The knocker was a lion head. She grabbed it and rapped the door three times.

The screen door didn't bang as she let it go and moved

back to the edge of the porch steps. Nothing happened. If anyone was home, they had to be asleep, but she guessed the house was empty.

Sarah opened the screen door and tried the knocker again. She hit it five times to make sure if anyone were asleep, they'd be awake now.

The farmhouse had old storm windows. The last time she'd seen windows like these was back in a cabin she was held in over four years ago. Her captor, Gert, had tried to use screws to seal the windows shut. Unless these windows were locked or sealed shut, she should be able to just raise them.

She tried the two front ones, but they didn't budge. Being careful to keep watching for an approaching vehicle, she walked around the house, trying all the windows.

When she got to the back of the house, the window leading into the kitchen lifted with ease. She pushed it up and lifted herself onto the sill. With a slight wince, both legs swung around and into the kitchen. She hopped off and dropped down to the tile floor.

"Ouch!" she muttered under her breath. "Damn, does that hurt."

She leaned on the counter and took in her surroundings. The place looked lived in. People had been here recently. Which meant they could be back at any time. She looked for a phone but couldn't find one in the kitchen. She walked into a hallway and then into the living room, being careful to remain quiet. No phones could be seen anywhere.

Maybe they didn't have phone access this far out. That reminded her that she had no idea where she was. She had been blindfolded on the way in. All she knew was how long the ride had been.

She was pretty sure the house was empty at the moment, but she needed to be certain. The stairs were off the hallway. On each step, she tested for creaks while watching above her. At the top, three open doors looked like bedrooms, and one was a bathroom. After a look at each bedroom, she relaxed. All the beds were made, and no one was home. The only fear was if the occupants came home while she was still inside. Although, on second thought, let them call the police. Maybe that would be the best option.

She entered the bathroom and turned on the shower. Hot water came quickly. She disrobed, removing her filthy, disgusting clothes, and hopped in.

Five minutes later, clean but in pain from the water hitting her wounds, Sarah walked into one of the bedrooms and opened a closet door. It was empty except for a few boxes. She went into the other bedroom and couldn't find any clothes there either.

Don't let me find an empty home so I can shower but not get new clothes. I will not put those shitty clothes on again.

In the last bedroom, the master suite, she opened the closet to reveal a large wardrobe of men's clothing.

With a quick check of sizes, she found a slim pair of track pants that would fit because they had a tie strap she could adjust. A clean white undershirt and a collared shirt to go over that got her dressed fast. She ran back to the bathroom and grabbed her running shoes. Most of the dirt came off them when she'd walked through the foliage, but she brushed off the remainder and slipped into them. With a final look in the mirror, she was ready to go.

She stopped cold and stared.

The collar shirt she now wore had a rip in it at the base.

What was this place? Who did these clothes belong to?

An engine revved outside. A car pulled up out front.

She ran to the bedroom that looked out onto the front lawn. Four black SUVs pulled into the driveway.

Her heart sank. They'd found her.

She bolted back to the bathroom and gathered up her dirty clothes. She brushed the remaining pieces of dirt under the bathroom carpet. As she raced out of the bathroom, she caught sight of the frosted mirror. She turned back and wiped it as fast as she could.

How was she going to remove the water from inside the bathtub? With no time left, she closed the shower curtain and ran from the bathroom.

It took her a few seconds to find the attic door in the roof of the second bedroom. She set her clothes down, brought an end table over, and stood on it to push the wood up into the attic. It lifted with ease. Before thinking about how she could get herself up and in, she tossed her dirty clothes through the hole, so at least they were out of the way.

The front door opened below her. Voices of multiple men rode the staircase to her.

She got off the end table and ran around the bed to the other one. It was heavy, but she managed to lift it and quietly move to the end of the bed.

Then she ran back to the one under the attic door, and even though her arm had a bullet wound, she used every last bit of strength to lift herself up and into the attic.

Someone ascended the stairs, pounding their footsteps hard.

There was no way she could move the end tables back into place. She'd felt it would be better to have two misplaced nightstands than just one. It wouldn't look good that the only one out of place just happened to be sitting under the attic door.

Now two people were at the top of the stairs. They were discussing a cop—someone making a trade of some kind.

She maneuvered the wooden attic cover and eased it back into place. It dropped with a soft thud.

"What was that?" one of the men asked.

The men in the upstairs hallway ran into the bedroom below her. She crawled backward, making every effort to be soft and quiet.

"I thought I heard a thump."

"Where?"

"In here."

"There's no one here, John."

"I can see that, asshole. What happened to these end tables?"

"I have no idea. Maybe someone moved them."

"Are you being a smart ass, Lenny? Because I could get really fucking angry if you are. Obviously, when I say I heard a noise, I did. And end tables don't move on their own."

"Okay, okay, take it easy. I'm just saying there's no one around for miles, and the house was locked, so there's no one here. We'd know the second we walked in if someone was here."

Sarah hoped that the second guy's logic won the first guy over.

I could really use a break here.

She lay completely still, listening, waiting.

"Come on, let's put these end tables back and get changed. We have a long day ahead of us."

Sarah heard them slide the end tables back beside the bed. With the soft patter of their feet, she heard both men leave the room. She let out the breath she'd been holding and started breathing more regularly.

Sarah checked out her new digs using what little light was available to her. There weren't any walls, just the underside of the ceiling as it joined in a V formation above her head. Pink insulation was jammed in between the studs haphazardly. The area she inhabited had a wooden base, big enough to spread out but hard as a rock. It had a thick layer of dust covering it. If she moved too fast, a cloud of it floated by. That ran the risk of causing her to sneeze or cough.

Four moving boxes were piled in a corner about five feet from her. She considered looking at them but decided to wait until the men below were either all downstairs, gone, or asleep.

A gentle move to the right got her farther from the attic access door, where she placed her old, dirty clothes. The smell bothered her more than before because she had spent most of the morning walking and breathing in the clean, fresh air. To be back in a confined space and smelling that shit again was just wrong.

She eased a little farther away and lay down to rest and think.

Now what? She escaped the compound only to walk right into their lair. She had no phone, no way to contact the outside world, and no idea where she was.

People were walking around in the upstairs area below her. The sound of distant voices traveled to her. A toilet flushed. Someone shouted something. Someone laughed.

Then she heard Sam Johnson's name. Why would they be

talking about Sam? She paid more attention, trying to listen to what they were saying.

The voices were too far away, but she was sure she heard the words "trade" and "kill him."

Chapter 26

Sam parked in the spot they told him to.

He took out his cell phone and texted Parkman his whereabouts. Maybe after he was taken, his colleagues could check the mall cameras for a hint as to who took him. Although, that would be futile, as these miscreants wouldn't have chosen a mall setting if they were worried about their faces on security cameras.

The dash clock read 10:01 a.m. He was a minute late.

Sam unclipped his holster and placed it under the front passenger seat with the gun. He touched his leg and felt for the knife. It was exactly where it was supposed to be.

Mall patrons walked by as he exited his vehicle, oblivious to the danger. He followed them into the mall.

His instructions had been simple. Walk to the maintenance doors by the JCPenney and then to the garbage compactor at the back. A garbage truck would be there to pick him up.

He located the JCPenney, walked by it, and opened the

maintenance door without a problem. The hallway was long and barren. He got to the compactor and saw a red door leading to the outside. He opened it and waited.

As if on cue, a large garbage truck came into view and lumbered up to him. A single driver wearing a black bandanna and sunglasses nodded at him.

Sam stepped onto the rungs on the passenger side and looked in the open window.

"Get in," the driver said.

"Where are Caleb and Amelia?"

"You get nothing until you get in."

Sam opened the door and sat down in the passenger seat. The garbage truck started moving right away. He waited. A deal was a deal. All he could hope for was they would honor their part in it.

The driver did not leave the mall's parking lot. Instead, he swung around and aimed for the area where Sam had parked. The driver applied the brakes and stopped four rows away from Sam's car.

"The parents are over there," the driver said, pointing.

A black SUV sat across the lot. The doors opened. Amelia, followed by Caleb, stepped out into the sunlight. They looked disheveled and disorientated.

The garbage truck driver reached down and lifted a device from the seat beside him. He looked over and smirked as he pushed a button on the device.

The explosion made the garbage truck sway. Instinctively, Sam shut his eyes and shielded his face. The first thought he had was Caleb and Amelia had been fitted with explosives, but when he looked through the truck's windshield, he saw that it was his car that had exploded. It was completely engulfed in flames, along with the two cars on either side.

Caleb and Amelia had taken shelter behind the SUV they'd just gotten out of.

Sam looked at the driver. "You're insane. Innocents could've gotten hurt."

He shook his head in the negative. "No, we're not insane. How do we know if you have a tracking device on your car? Maybe you left a message in there for someone about this plan. I'm sure you won't need your car anymore, anyway. You knew this was a one-way trip when you signed on."

"You keep telling yourself that," Sam muttered.

He looked for Sarah's parents again and saw they had run away from the parking lot. They were crossing the street and heading to an office building.

They were moving toward safety.

The driver got underway. Fifteen minutes later, they exited the city limits. Flat grassland and the odd batch of trees passed by as they cruised just under the speed limit.

They'd done a pretty stupid thing by having just a driver with him. The guy hadn't even frisked him yet.

He looked in the rearview mirror. Two black SUVs that resembled the one from the mall were following close.

Of course.

It took them no time at all to pull over and get rid of the garbage truck. Sam was ordered into the second SUV. He and the garbage truck driver climbed into the back seat. Then they were underway again.

The front passenger pulled out a long strip of black cloth. The driver shook his head. The passenger shrugged and put the cloth away. No blindfold? That wasn't a good start.

It crossed his mind to try to take out as many of these guys as he could and then run for it. He'd already saved Sarah's parents, so he could take off. But he remained quiet and waited. It was Sarah, Esmerelda, and Dolan that he was after. He wanted to know where they were, and then he would find a way to finish this.

Even if it cost him his life.

Exhaustion clung to him as they drove the endless highway, his eyes heavy. Parkman had gotten him up early to meet at that truck stop, and now he was feeling the effects of it. No one spoke. One man sat beside him with two in the front. He needed conversation to wake up.

"Do all of you guys have a twin complex?"

No one responded. The man beside him continued looking forward.

"You all drive the same black SUV and wear the same black jackets. You all rip the bottoms of your shirts. Why is that?"

The guy beside him looked out the window as if something interesting caught his attention.

"Does a great personality go with the job as well?" Sam asked.

They pulled off the highway and started up a winding dirt road. He hadn't seen a house or any sign of civilian life for quite some time.

The SUV pulled up and stopped in front of a barn-like structure attached to a much larger building. He wondered if that was where they kept a getaway plane.

The men got out and walked around to Sam's door. It was opened, and he stepped out. An older man approached and took off his glasses.

"We will dispense with the niceties," the old man said. "I have paid a steep price for having you join us today. Please, come with me so we can begin our conversation." The man turned and gestured with his hands toward the barn doors.

"Niceties?" Sam asked. "Am I in the right place? I think they missed my stop along the way. I'm supposed to meet a bunch of thugs and a bad guy who kidnaps little girls."

The old man turned and met Sam's eyes. His face was rugged from years in the sun, but to Sam, it looked like a face of stone.

"Don't humor yourself with games, Mr. Johnson. I assure you, my men will kill you where you stand. I can only keep the ravenous grizzly caged for so long. Won't you join me?" He gestured toward the barn again.

Sam looked at the men scattered behind him. Two of them reached inside their jackets, implying a weapon was in their hands. Not sure how this would turn out, he started toward the barn door knowing that he may have to act at any second.

He followed the old man down a hallway and into a room. One table and one chair sat in the middle, with a solitary light dangling above the table.

This must be their interrogation room.

The old man said, "My friend, Blake, and his associate, have a few questions for you. After that, you will be made comfortable providing you answer correctly. I bid you farewell."

The door shut behind him, leaving the three men standing in the dank room looking at each other.

Sam addressed the one called Blake. "So, do you guys ask the questions or me?"

He watched as Blake reached inside his jacket and pulled out a whip.

"Okay, is this where it gets serious?" Sam asked. "This is your interrogation room, right? Interrogate me, then. What have I got to lose? I'm captive here with no idea where I am, so there's no need to have a show of violence. I'll talk. Or rather, we can talk. Fire away."

The associate pulled out a gun. He cocked the hammer. "Fire away?" he said.

"Wait, wait—"

The gun coughed. Sam felt a tear below the knee. The bullet hit hard, knocking his leg out from under him. He lost his balance and dropped to the floor.

The pain wasn't what hit him first. It was the shock of being shot. He heard his scream start as a frustrated wail, turning into something more painful.

Blood oozed out of the wound in the center of his calf muscle.

"What the *fuck*!" he screamed.

The guy with the whip smiled. Sam already forgot his name. Something about that guy freaked him out. Some men acted the part. Some wanted to be tough. A guy like him was just evil. It came off him in waves.

"I wanted to talk," Sam managed to say. "I even said ..." Sam tried to calm his breathing. He looked at his leg. The bullet had gone right through. A glance at the floor three feet behind him confirmed it. There was a small indent on the floor where the bullet made contact after going through his leg.

When he looked back up, the guy with the whip moved toward him. In a flash, he dove, landing on Sam, wrestling him down, the strap flailing in the air. The pain in his leg worsened. He had no strength to fight the guy off. The pain became excruciating.

Then he passed out.

Chapter 27

SHE HADN'T HEARD ANY noises for some time. She had strained to hear more of their conversations to glean anything on Sam Johnson or what they meant by "trade" and "kill him," but couldn't.

She angled her body up so she could crawl. If someone had thought to put a window in the attic, it might not be so hot. Sarah brushed at the sweat on her forehead as it kept threatening to blind her. The act of a miscalculation, a misstep, could spell disaster. If she tumbled to the side and dropped hard to the attic floor, it would surely alert the men below.

So with each movement, she tested it and then eased into the next one. It took her a full three minutes to cross five feet. At the boxes, she unclipped one and took a look inside. Old blankets and what looked like tablecloths were folded and placed neatly inside.

She moved to her right and opened another box. Inside were school supplies. Empty binders and textbooks filled it.

Before closing the lid and moving to the next box, something caught her eye. She looked back in and confirmed her suspicion—a pencil case. It came free without protest. She shook it. A writing tool lay within. She opened the zipper and pulled out a red pencil crayon.

Her arm went numb.

She had a couple of seconds to secure herself before passing out.

What am I going to write on? she thought as she passed out.

***

People were in the room below her as she stirred awake. Something was burning, too. Maybe they screwed something up in the kitchen.

The pencil crayon wasn't in her hand anymore. She looked around, but it was gone.

What's that smell? What could they have been cooking to cause it to reek so badly?

The two boxes she had opened remained that way. She could see no sign of paper anywhere. Perhaps she didn't write anything this time. Although that would be unusual, as she did pass out with a writing tool in her hand, the only time that happens is when a message comes through.

The smell in the attic became unbearable.

Someone pounded down the steps below, yelling something unintelligible. It sounded like they said it was "set" and "everyone out."

But why leave when they're cooking?

It didn't matter. If they were leaving, she could too. She

moved with stealth to sit right over the top of the wooden access door to the attic. The burning smell grew stronger here.

They didn't set the house on fire, did they?

She had a sidelong view of the four moving boxes from her position above the attic door. One of the boxes she'd opened had something on the side of it. She edged closer. Sure enough, it was as she'd suspected. The writing was in red pencil crayon. Why hadn't she thought to look at the boxes?

The words chilled her even though they were a mystery.

... hide when wet ... kill to save a life ...

What the hell did that mean? Hide when wet? When was she going to be wet? And, of course, she would kill to save a life, but kill who and save who?

She answered precognitions to save lives. When she started on this path, it gave her power and a sense of worth that her childhood hadn't offered. She felt empowered with the knowledge of the future. The fact that she wielded the ability to change the future and save lives thrust her into these ventures, so killing was out of the question.

But she would do it to save lives.

Always to save lives.

The burning smell gagged her. She coughed involuntarily. One last look at the message, and she scurried back to the wooden access door.

She had to open the attic door or be killed by the smoke filling the crawlspace.

Her fingers gripped the edge of the wood. Being careful to do it quietly, Sarah lifted the wood and looked down. The room was empty directly below her, except for the smoke.

If the house was on fire, she was in trouble. The implication of her receiving another message earlier meant she would live through this unless the *kill to save a life* part had something to do with her death. She refused to believe that. She would live through this.

She placed both hands on the edge of the square attic door frame, palm down. She ducked her head down first and brought her hips to her hands to prepare for an inverted roll. Then she dropped her butt through the hole, and her legs followed as she unrolled herself into a hanging position. With only three feet to the floor, she let go of the frame and dropped into the room, taking the weight onto her good leg.

Instantly, she knelt to her knees to get below the smoke. In the hall outside the room, smoke rolled up from downstairs.

The house was on fire. There was no question about it.

Sarah moved to the bedroom door and looked out. No one was on this floor. Black smoke rose from the stairwell.

She ran to the window in the bedroom. One black SUV was just pulling away. It hit the road at the end of the driveway and turned right, where it raced off.

The last SUV still sat in front of the house, but she couldn't see anyone. She coughed, then coughed again. She could hear the flames licking at something downstairs.

The window had a small latch halfway up. She undid the latch and opened it. As fast as smoke filtered out, fresh air was close enough to get a few gulps. She closed her eyes and breathed it in to fill her lungs.

Then the window shattered above her. She jumped back so fast that she lost her balance and landed hard on her ass in the center of the room.

Angered voices screamed from below. The remaining SUV driver and passenger must have walked out toward their vehicle to leave and either heard her or seen her at the window.

Sarah crept closer to the sill and listened.

"She's in the house!"

"I know, but we can't go back in. It's too late now. Leave it. She'll die in the fire."

"Or maybe I hit her when I shot at the window. She did jump back like she was hit."

Sarah muffled a cough with her sleeve. Fear can play an active role in decision-making. It told her to haul ass, but she resisted, wanting to hear as much as possible.

"I'm waiting here until the house collapses. What if she walks away from this?"

"She won't walk away. I'm going to be in the car. I'll call in and tell them we found the girl and that she's going to burn in the house. I'll wait for you there."

That was all Sarah needed.

She got up and rushed from the room. She found a couple of towels draped over the shower curtain in the bathroom. She turned on the shower head and ran them under the water, surprised and happy the water still ran.

The note said *hide when wet,* so maybe this was it. Leaving the water running, she wrapped one of the towels around her shoulders, and the other she laid atop her head. Cool water dripped into her ears. She felt a stir of hope in a moment's reprieve from the rising heat.

The bathroom was an enclosed space and rapidly filling with smoke. She could almost feel the heat rising through her shoes. She ran away from the stairs where the fire was licking up the handrail and back into the room with the open window.

Without exposing herself, she leaned in close and sucked at the fresh air, coughed, and then sucked some more.

The guy with the gun outside was singing.

"The roof, the roof, the roof, is on fire. We don't need no water. Let the motherfucker burn!"

A nagging feeling of panic struck and wouldn't let go. The house shifted under her. She felt it move, and her will to survive surged with it. Being on the second floor of a burning house was madness.

Hide when wet.

She was wet and hiding.

Kill to save a life.

She would love to kill the bastard downstairs, but how? How could she get down there and not get killed in the process?

The air from the window was so sweet she didn't want to leave it. Allowing one more long inhale, Sarah got up, left the room, and ran to the top of the stairs. It was the only way down.

But it was too late.

The stairs, banister, and the entire bottom were completely engulfed in fire. As she watched, the bottom of the stairs collapsed. The heat was unbearable. She moved back.

There was nowhere to go, no way out.

Interpreting the message correctly, she had hidden when wet, but there was no one to kill.

Trapped in a burning house that was falling apart around her, smoke rising to cut off her oxygen, she screamed at the futility of it. She screamed at the injustice. But most of all, she was yelling because she didn't want to die this way, to be accidentally caught and killed by the scum downstairs.

Then the floor under the bathroom and the room under the attic collapsed with a huge bang and an enormous amount of smoke.

It would only be a matter of minutes before the hallway she was in would fall, too.

Sarah prayed and wept.

Chapter 28

PARKMAN STRUGGLED TO QUELL his anger. The car door stuck as he attempted to get out. He fumbled with the handle, got it open, and almost fell out.

"Shit!" he yelled.

With his siren on, he had squealed into the mall parking lot, and now a small crowd stared at him.

The place was sealed off as a crime scene in two areas. Parkman saw the bomb disposal crew packing up, crime scene detectives working the scene, and FBI agents standing around in their suits, talking with each other. Dozens of pedestrians stood at various spots behind the police tape, gawking at the live edition of CSI.

He spotted Special Agent Jill Hanover immediately as she waved at him. He kept telling himself the anger he felt was justified. Someone had to be held accountable for these mistakes.

And it was a terrible time to be out of toothpicks.

"Parkman, good to see you here," Hanover said.

"Wouldn't miss it," he said as he walked up.

"Do I detect a hint of something in your voice?" She widened her eyes, waited for a second, and then slit them in her over-dominating way.

He stared back at her and gave no response. She took that as her cue to go on.

"We have Caleb and Amelia," Hanover said. "But they won't talk to us."

"I wonder why?"

"What's that?"

"I said, I wonder why."

Hanover rushed Parkman, coming up nose to nose with him.

"I don't like this any more than you do," she said. "I didn't ask to be kept out of the loop. Sam did this on his own. Now, I've asked you to come back on the team because the Roberts clan refuses to talk to us. We need your help. If you don't want to help, then fuck off!"

She stepped back and crossed her arms.

Parkman turned around to walk away. Her hand grabbed his shoulder and swung him back.

"Where're you going?" Hanover demanded.

"To talk to the Robertses. Isn't that why you asked me to be here?" He tried hard but couldn't keep the distaste for Hanover off his face. He knew she couldn't just see it. She could feel it, too.

Sam could've been killed here today. The Roberts were freed in exchange for a good cop, and no one knew anything about it. Even the mighty FBI was clueless.

This case was fucked from the beginning. Possibly Parkman could've done something to help if he had not been treated like their personal yo-yo with a badge.

He turned away from Hanover and walked down a line of FBI vehicles. At the end of the line, Caleb and Amelia Roberts sat in a black Suburban. Parkman showed his ID to the agent guarding the SUV and stepped in.

"They drag you out to talk to us?" Caleb asked.

"How are you two doing? I can't imagine how tough this has been."

Caleb looked at his wife and then back to Parkman. "We're okay but concerned. I remember something like this playing out four years ago. That time we almost didn't get our daughter back. What guarantees do we have this time?"

Parkman looked at both of them and then out the side window. Before turning back, he reached for the toothpick in his mouth only to remember that he didn't have one.

"Unfortunately, there are no guarantees. But I assure you I will do everything possible to fix this."

"I see we have the same FBI team working on this as the last time. They weren't effective then. What's different now?"

Six bottles of water were stacked neatly in a holder by the door. Parkman gestured, and after Caleb nodded, he grabbed one.

"The only thing different is me. I will work this. Sam will work this. You know that Sam was the only one who was the closest to helping Sarah last time. He's on the inside now."

Caleb frowned and leaned back in the leather seat.

Parkman dropped his head and looked at the floor. Then he glanced at Amelia. She was staring outside at the commotion happening beyond them near the burned-out vehicle. She appeared to not be listening, but Parkman knew better.

"Caleb, Sam, and I will do everything we can to get Sarah home safe. She's our top priority."

"No one can help Sarah, Parkman. You, of all people, know her. She's resourceful. She'll get herself out before anyone else will be able to. She doesn't trust cops, so I don't see how you lot can help. They want us to tell them everything, and for what? So they can fill a file somewhere. Forget it."

"Sarah trusts Sam," Parkman continued. "She trusts me, too—"

"You know the profiles of criminals like these. You know the probability of Sam walking away from this is low. I'm sorry, but no one is coming home safe unless a miracle happens. They have Esmerelda, Dolan, Sarah, and now Sam. We were told that if we helped the police in any way, Sarah would be the first to die."

"Is that why you won't talk to Agent Hanover or her team?"

Caleb looked at his wife. "Sarah walked into this, as far as I understand. She gets those messages from Vivian. Vigilantism has always bothered us, but Sarah is twenty-two now. We can't stop her. If her sister walked her into this, then her sister would get her out. I'd put my money on Sarah and her sister working this out on their own."

"You have a lot of faith in the dead. I'm sorry if I come across as crass, but if someone from the Other Side is helping her, then why not just tell us what's happening, and we'll arrest the criminals?"

"It doesn't work like that for Sarah, and you know it. It's

personal for her. It always has been. Remember where she gets her messages—from a blood relative who was raped and murdered twenty years ago. She's gotta be pretty pissed off about that. It seems to me that Vivian gets to live through Sarah, and Sarah lives through Vivian."

Parkman was still holding the bottle of water. He uncapped it and took a swig. "Is there *anything* you can tell me?"

"They blindfolded us each way. The ride was direct, with not too many turns. It lasted at least an hour. That's all I know. We were held in little rooms, like small sheds, until they came and blindfolded us again and brought us here. That's it."

"Can you tell me anything else?"

"We've said all we can."

Parkman looked at Amelia and then back to Caleb. "I imagine you'll be in custody until this thing blows over?"

"According to Hanover, yes, that is the case."

"Okay, I'll be in touch."

They nodded, and Parkman stepped from the Suburban.

He headed directly to his car. Hanover hollered behind him.

"Wait up!" she yelled.

He got to his car and turned around. She was twenty feet behind him.

"What did they say?" Hanover asked. "You're just going to leave?"

"They said nothing. They're sworn to secrecy, or Sarah dies."

He felt Hanover's eyes on him, appraising whether he was telling her the truth.

"I gotta go," Parkman said and opened his door.

"Wait. Where are you going?"

"To figure this thing out. To find Sarah and Sam."

"Not without us, you aren't."

"Watch me."

Parkman dropped into his vehicle and squealed out of the parking lot, knowing he was probably leaving his job behind.

One last glimpse at Hanover, and he could see she was already talking into her lapel microphone, probably telling someone to tail him.

He broke the speed limit and circled a few city blocks for thirty minutes to make sure no one was following him and then hit the highway in search of some kind of compound with small sheds that was an hour's drive away.

Chapter 29

Bent over, Sarah rushed into the master bedroom and closed the door behind her in a feeble attempt to keep the smoke out.

The bedroom window opened easily. What little smoke had made it into this room before she shut the door billowed out as she sucked at the air from the outside. This room had a bed, two night tables, and a small desk. She walked over and opened the closet to survey the clothes.

Something banged in the house somewhere, startling her. The door buckled from the heat, and smoke forced itself under it.

She spied a man's leather belt on the shelf above the hangers. It would have to do. Maybe if she somehow secured it to the window, the few feet it offered would be enough for her to jump without breaking an ankle or a leg. Her choice was either a jump from the second-story window or stay inside the house and burn with it.

Dizziness threatened to overcome her as she felt

lightheaded from the smoke she had already inhaled. The cough was back, but she was at the window a moment later, belt in hand.

She looked down at the ground below the back bedroom window and then wanted to smack herself for forgetting.

The pool.

It was a circular above-ground pool with a cover. It was still filled with water. She had walked right by it when looking for a way into the house.

How could I've forgotten?

It took her no time at all to crawl onto the window sill. She wrapped the belt around her right wrist and sat there for a second, judging the distance and how she wanted to land.

The house made more noises behind her as she hovered in the window.

Hide when wet ... kill to save a life ...

That must be what it meant. When she hit the pool, she would hide as the men in the front of the house investigated what noise she had made. The life to save would be hers.

That meant it was time to kill some bad guys.

She counted to three and pushed off the sill.

Chapter 30

Sam heard the smack as much as he felt it.

He rose back up to his own nightmare. The pain aided his return to consciousness. When he opened his eyes, the gunman was sitting on the table, and the guy with the whip was standing over him, rubbing the palm of his hand.

Blood still oozed from his leg, but it had slowed.

Why bring him out here just to kill him? He reasoned they wouldn't make a trade for the Roberts if all they wanted to do was kill an evidence clerk from the police station.

His leg throbbed where the bullet had punctured. The strap was wrapped around his leg above the thigh. It had been pulled snug into what looked like a decent field-dressing tourniquet.

The man with the gun said, "You probably know how this works. Help us, and you die quickly, don't help us, and you die slowly. That strap on your leg is the only one my friend has, so there will be no more tourniquets. Are we clear?"

Sam nodded, already deducing how he could get to them. The Whip Man moved back by the door, and the gunman stood a few feet away by the table. With a bad leg, he couldn't rush them without getting hit by another bullet. It all would come down to a science. Where the bullet hit would determine if he got to the guy or not. If he got close enough, his knife would be aimed for the jugular in the guy's throat.

"What do the police know about us? Bring us up to speed. Tell us about the case."

Sam grunted as he rolled over. It may have looked like he was favoring his injured leg, but he was angling himself to get better access to the knife.

"What *do* the police know?" Sam echoed.

"Don't repeat the questions. Just answer them."

He got into the best position he could find that gave him good access to his knife and allowed his wounded leg to rest with no pressure on it. Below the hip, he was rapidly becoming numb, which was a good thing, for he needed to think clearly to increase the odds of taking them out.

The gunman stepped closer. "We're running out of time. Start talking, or we won't need you anymore."

Sam raised a hand. "Okay, okay, no need to shoot me again. I'll talk. Just give me a second."

"There's no time left. Tell us what the police know."

"We know about the kidnappings. The police know that you have Esmerelda, Dolan, and Sarah."

"What else?"

The gunman stood close, holding his weapon aimed down at the floor.

"We know that anyone associated with this group, whoever you are, has a rip at the base of their shirt." Sam looked over at Whip Man. Because of the way he was standing, the rip showed easily. "Like that one." He pointed.

"I need to know if the FBI has any idea where we are at the moment. What is their progress? Tell us something useful. Patience, I haven't got much of."

"They believe your group is responsible for the two dead cops."

"That was unfortunate. Those traffic cops got involved in something they shouldn't have."

Sam eased his leg to the side and scrunched his face at the pain. "Batches of license plates were stolen from the same neighborhood. We believe those are the plates you guys use on all your SUVs. Hey, look, could I get some water?"

The gunman shook his head. "No water."

"Fucking idiot," Sam muttered.

"What was that?"

"I said, I haven't been working directly with the FBI, but I know Jill Hanover is in charge. I also suspect they know that Jack Tate is somehow involved with you because his shirt was ripped, and the dead girl found by his house had to be his victim."

"No, not his. The dead girl was planted there. The FBI has been getting close to Jack, watching him. He had us plant the body to shine less light on him as a suspect. The ripped shirt on the girl was an oversight. He was pretty pissed we fucked that up, eh Blake?"

Blake nodded.

"Why tell me that?" Sam asked. "When I leave here, I'll have to report what you said."

"Leave here? You know, Sam, you're a riot. What else do you have?"

Sam leaned back and sprawled flat on the floor, getting comfortable and ready for what was coming. "We know about a recent kidnapping in another State. The girl was spotted here locally. Since you guys are in the area, I think the FBI has put it together that she's been taken by your group." He stopped and looked sideways up at the gunman. "Let me ask you something. What do you guys call yourself, and is this all just a ruse for human trafficking?"

"Do you have any guesses?"

"I know that whatever it is, it's completely crazy. You can't kill cops and not expect a manhunt."

"That's why we're moving shop. We'll be halfway across the country within days. But enough about that. What else can you tell us?"

"I was a loner on this case. I kept hitting a wall. So at this point, I don't have anything else." He moved so he'd get better access to the knife. When he was shot earlier, the bullet ripped open his pant leg two inches from the knife. The tourniquet was an inch above that. Sam had no idea how they missed the blade when the tourniquet was tied.

"Are you saying you don't know that Sarah Roberts escaped?"

He jerked his head up in surprise. "What? Sarah escaped? When?"

"That's not important. As we searched for her, we decided to trade you for her parents to see what the cops knew. As we can see, they don't know much more than we thought. At least they have no idea what we're doing. Sarah must've never made it to society. It's a long walk."

"What *are* you doing?"

The gunman addressed Blake. "You see, Blake, they are

stupid. Our operation isn't in jeopardy. Go take care of the rest of the prisoners. We won't be needing them anymore. Then come back here to help me dispose of Sam's body. Reassure our investors that all is well in the Nation. Then we need to move the remaining girls to the new compound."

Blake opened the door and stepped out, closing it firmly behind him.

"Girls? New compound?"

"Yes, Sam. This is all about girls. Young girls, born to be sluts, really."

The gunman showed him his back. The magazine in the gun unclipped. He was checking his weapon, getting it ready for use.

Sam reached into the hole in his pants, said a quick prayer, and yanked the blade free.

The door opened.

"We found Sarah." It was the guy with the black glasses that Sam had met earlier as he got out of the SUV. "You won't believe where."

Sam clutched the knife in his palm, the blade angled down by his wrist. It was completely out of sight of both men.

"Tell me," the gunman said.

"In our resting home. Can you believe it?"

"Did they kill her?"

"They didn't know she was even there until they set the house on fire. Luke saw her in a window and shot at her. He's staying behind until he's sure she's dead."

House on fire! Sam prayed Sarah would make it. He knew she'd been in worse situations and walked away. Even a burning building hadn't stopped her before.

"That's crazy," the gunman said, smiling. "What are the odds she'd show up there?"

"We're all ready to go. Finish up here, and we'll leave in thirty minutes."

They nodded at each other, and the guy with the glasses stepped back out.

"You were saying how this is all about girls," Sam said. "What were you talking about?"

The gunman looked at him. Then he nodded. "I've got a few minutes, so I'll humor you. We're an extension of a larger group that brings girls in from all over the world, the U.S. included, for the rich and elite. Some of us have been at this for many years. Armond, or as you know him, Jack Tate, started the group way back when he was a cop. It began as a massage parlor in the seventies and then transitioned to a condo, and finally, it escalated to Armond picking up girls that clients specifically requested."

So it was true. Jack Tate was Armond Stuart. "Requested girls? How does that work?"

"Certain men have a taste that's hard to satisfy. Armond would go all over the States to get what they wanted at a price. He got rich fast, but ultimately he needed help."

"Is Armond Jack Tate's real name?"

"No one knows his real name, but that doesn't matter now."

The gunman clipped the weapon's safety off and aimed it at Sam.

Sam shuddered. "So basically, you guys are all pimps. Glorified whores. What's next, male prostitutes?"

He needed to say something to keep the guy talking, something that might jar him. The gun faltered and lowered again.

"No, it isn't that simple. We offer a service. Some of the richest men in the world pay us to enjoy the benefits of sleeping with a girl at any age they request with complete anonymity. We have no restrictions other than confidentiality. Our rule is, break that, and your price is one of your children. If you have no children, then we castrate you and leave your snitch ass maimed for life. Break confidentiality twice, instant death. That's it. Pay your bill, have fun, keep your mouth shut, and walk away clean. Our clients respect that."

Sam pushed back and leaned his upper body against the wall. "You do know how crazy that is, right?"

"No, not crazy, genius. It's something that men worldwide are already doing but with greater risk. Pay the right price and get whatever you want, risk-free—a solid business venture."

"Then why the psychics?" Sam asked. "Why run the risk of kidnapping people you won't use and killing cops, too?"

"Oh, we use psychics all the time. We kidnap at least two to three psychics annually to have on staff. Armond believes in them. They help us find the right girls we're looking for and let us know when our risk factor increases with the authorities. They're disposed of when they refuse to help or simply can't anymore. Sam, the only people who get out of here alive, are the ones who pay money to enter. That's it."

"That's human trafficking *and* murder. It sounds to me like you guys have killed a lot of people." Sam gritted his teeth and pushed against the wall on his good leg to stand. "But what you just said begs another question. If the only people who leave here are the ones who have money, then am I right to assume that if I paid a certain amount of money, it would secure my release?"

The gunman shook his head. "Sam, I said, the only ones are the people who *pay* to *enter*. Not pay to negotiate their release. Although I assure you, you'll leave this compound. Only it'll be in a body bag."

"Not if I can help it," Sam said and reached his full height using the wall. A dizzy spell came and went.

"What do you mean, *not if I can help it*?" the gunman asked as he stepped closer.

Sam coughed himself into a fit, bent over. He stopped for a second, eyes watering, and leaned back up. He intimated that he wanted to say something but couldn't. The gunman wasn't close enough. He bent over and coughed more.

"I want …" Sam tried and then coughed into his arm. When he spoke next, he made it soft and raspy. It came out unintelligible.

"I have no idea what you're saying, Sam, but your time is up. Say your piece, and then I have to go."

Sam gestured for the gunman to come closer. He was hoping he wouldn't faint. His strength was leaving him. One more attempt at speaking, and the gunman stepped close enough to touch.

Sam raised his empty hand and beckoned.

With as much speed as he could muster, Sam lunged with his right hand, the large blade exposed now.

It sliced at least an inch deep into the gunman's throat before he knew what hit him. His eyes widened in surprise.

Sam let out a sigh of relief as the gun fell to the floor. Most professionals would've still taken the shot at Sam as they died, but not this guy. He was too stunned that Sam had knifed him.

In less than a minute, the gunman's body lay still in the pool of blood that had grown to circle his head and shoulders. He died with his eyes wide open. Sam left them that way.

They can dry right out of your fucking head, asshole.

Sam picked up the gun, feeling the cold steel and weight of the weapon. A rush of adrenaline flowed through him, making it feel like he was on a Red-Bull high. He limped to the door and looked outside. Deep, regular breaths had dispelled the wooziness, keeping it at bay.

The hall beyond the door was empty. He left the gunman's body in the empty room and started down the corridor in pursuit of Armond.

Today, he gave back to all the people the police couldn't protect.

Today he'd kill some bad guys.

Chapter 31

SARAH HIT THE POOL cover hard. It collapsed as water seeped in around her. Her legs broke the fall, with each shoulder taking the rest of the impact as she rolled onto the cover toward the edge of the pool.

The water was cold but refreshing. Her only hope was that it had been cleaned recently.

She had no way of knowing if they heard her hit the water as it engulfed her in its four feet of cold depth. She had managed to take a deep breath before being completely submerged.

The belt was still wrapped around her right wrist. In the water, on her back, she loosened it and wrapped it around her left wrist, too. Then she brought the belt's ends apart until it was taut.

The perfect garrote.

She looked up through the film of water and saw the house completely aflame. The window she had just jumped from had an orange light coming from it now. The window on the first floor was surrounded in black as the fire had licked through it for some time now.

She estimated she'd been upside down in the pool for half a minute. The water pushed her to rise to the surface, so she released air from her lungs and gently moved her legs to keep near the bottom. Within ten to fifteen seconds, she would have to surface.

A shadow crossed her vision. She stopped moving. Her lung's protest deepened. The little smoke she had inhaled earlier fought to get her to cough. Submerged as she was, she could hear her pulse in her ear now.

But she waited. Sometimes there were more important things to do than breathing. If she got up at the wrong time, she could be killed.

... hide when wet ...

The shadow passed the surface of the water again.

Sarah lowered her head down, chin touching chest, and looked at the guy who had shot at her when she was in the upstairs window. Nerves made her hands shake as her body filled with adrenaline.

The man had his back to her as he stared up at the burning house. Either the fire mesmerized his pyromaniacal delusions, or he was riveted by the fact that Sarah was supposed to be sticking her head out of a window at any moment in search of oxygen.

As slow as she could, disturbing the water as little as possible, Sarah eased to the surface. She broke the water and took a quiet, deep breath. She stayed low so as not to drip or make splashing noises.

Chance favors the prepared mind, she thought as the guy backed up toward the pool. *If he only knew ...*

He stopped a couple of feet in front of her.

She took two deep breaths and then held the last one. Then Sarah brought the belt up and around the guy's throat and yanked him back. Her feet slipped, causing her to fall back into the pool. The goon fell with her. Normally, a man his size would knock the wind out of her, but the water softened his descent.

He didn't get a chance to breathe before the belt wrapped around his throat. As they dropped under the surface of the water, his hands grasped at the belt, trying frantically to release its grip.

Sarah pulled it tighter as they hit the bottom of the pool, hoping he would succumb before she needed to breathe again.

The water weakened his struggle. Then he slowed his fight and stopped, floating motionlessly above her. Sarah's chest pumped for air, but she held on to make sure he wasn't bluffing. She pulled on the belt harder still and waited a few more seconds until her chest felt like it was on fire. He remained a dead weight in the water. Convinced he was gone, her lungs about ready to burst, she eased his body off hers, and then she stood to breathe.

She glanced back down at him. He was dead. Only his partner remained to be dealt with.

The edge of the pool had to be straddled to get out. Even though it was around midday, the sun high and the day warm, she shivered when the air touched her.

The noise of the fire crackling was louder than she thought it would be. Or maybe that was because all she heard underwater had been her pulse.

Not three feet from the pool sat the guy's gun. The dead

guy must have had it in his hand when she grabbed him around the neck.

She picked it up. A Sig Sauer P226. A nice weapon used by police departments and the military.

What are these guys doing with such serious weapons?

Sarah popped the magazine release. Two bullets were missing. She popped it back in and released the safety.

In the backyard, twenty feet from her, a rock about the size of a softball sat in a tuft of grass. She grabbed it and ran close to the house, carefully watching for pieces of debris that might fall. This side of the house was upwind as the smoke rose away, leaving the exterior wall untouched.

At the front corner, she took extra care to go slow, edging around the corner until the SUV parked out front was in view. The driver sat behind the wheel. He was looking down, examining something on his lap.

Sarah threw the rock toward the SUV. Then she turned and ran in the opposite direction.

She cleared the back and ran around the pool. On the far side of the house, she held her breath and ran through the smoke, coming out on the other side of it, her eyes watering. Having almost completely circled the house, she slowed as the SUV was about to come into view again.

She planned to have the driver give chase or at least come to investigate who had thrown a rock at him. Sometimes the simple plans worked the best.

When she looked around the edge of the house, the SUV's front door sat open, the driver nowhere in sight. She hustled out from cover and jogged along the front of the burning house. She got to the corner where she had originally thrown the rock and jumped around it with the hopes of coming in behind the driver, the Sig raised and ready to fire.

But no one was there.

If the driver had looked in the pool, he would have seen his dead partner and known he was in danger, too. Had the tables turned? She had wanted to lure the driver out, but now she had no idea where he was.

With the amount of smoke the house emitted, someone was bound to see it and call the fire department soon. She had to locate the driver, execute or incapacitate him, and leave. Otherwise, she would never find the compound and lose the only people she cared about.

A shiver coursed through her. She had to think. To get around the house as fast as she did, the driver wouldn't have walked from the SUV and been lost to sight without her seeing him. Unless he ran to the back, and she just missed him. Or he was still in the SUV, in which case he would've seen her as she ran along the front of the house.

Something loud crashed behind her as the fire continued its assault on the building. Impulsively she stepped away from the wall. She looked left and right, watching each side in case the driver walked out.

Even outside the house, she was trapped now.

The driver's side door was still open, but there was no sign of the driver. Normally people close their doors when getting out of a vehicle, even if they're coming right back.

The open door was meant as an invitation. The driver either knew the rock thrower was Sarah or suspected it was.

Why would his partner throw a rock at him?

Stupid, stupid, stupid.

Why didn't he shoot her when she ran along the front of the house?

Because he would want a sure shot. One that was closer. As soon as she figured out he was gone, she would move on the open door of an empty SUV. That would be her mistake. Then he would pounce.

So now what?

Frustration made her grind her teeth as time ran out. The house was collapsing, and using it for cover would prove difficult very soon.

Maybe she should walk toward the vehicle and fire on him as soon as he popped his head up. But that was too risky. There had to be a better way.

Sarah screamed, yelling out her frustration. The anger in her rose, goading her to a fight. Before long, the scream took on a life of its own, making it sound like she was being bludgeoned. It brought goosebumps to her arms. Then, she clamped her mouth shut and fired two bullets into the side of the house.

She hoped her ruse would work. Would the driver think his partner had silenced her? Would he come out of hiding?

She waited, gun ready. After a slow, agonizing count to ten, she stepped around the corner of the house and into the open, the weapon held out in front of her.

The driver of the SUV stood ten feet away.

She stared at him.

He stared back.

Neither one said a word.

Fire licked the wall where Sarah had been moments before. The house burned as they waited to see who would move first.

Her eyes stayed still and true. They remained locked on his as his were on hers. Peripheral vision caught movement as his right thumb caressed the back of his gun.

But Sarah had won because hers was aimed at his throat while his was aimed at the ground. The delay helped her ensure she wouldn't miss with one shot.

She applied gentle pressure to the trigger.

The Sig spit in her hand, and a red dot formed on the driver's throat at the base of his neck, dead center.

In reaction to the noise, at the exact second her weapon fired, his gun hand had started to rise but stopped suddenly as he felt the punch in the center of his neck.

His hands covered the wound, his gun forgotten, dropped to the grass. His eyes widened as blood seeped past his fingers, and his life ebbed out in a liquid torrent.

He fell to his knees.

Sarah wasted no time. She strutted past him, only slowing to grab his gun, and continued to the SUV.

The keys were still there when she hopped into the driver's seat.

In seconds she had the vehicle turned around and racing down the same road the other SUV had taken earlier.

Chapter 32

AN HOUR OUT OF town and Parkman was already regretting how he'd handled Agent Hanover. He had no leads and no idea where to start. He couldn't even be sure if he'd taken the right highway out of town. There were at least four highways that allowed exit from the city.

The mall where the Roberts exchange took place was two miles from Route 9, leading into a flat-land area. Without overthinking it, Parkman had assumed this was the way the others would have traveled. He couldn't see the perps taking an extra hour driving through the city to get to the other side, where an exchange would occur at a mall. The risk of being seen or pulled over was too great, and the trip was too time-consuming.

Without a solid lead—or even a brittle one—he could drive this road for days and find nothing. He needed something, and Hanover was his lifeline whether he liked it or not. They were on the same side, and he preferred not to lose his career over this.

He dialed Hanover's number and waited while it rang on the hands-free.

"Agent Hanover."

"Hanover, it's Parkman."

"Where are you?"

"About an hour out of town."

"What are you doing out there?" Hanover asked. "Is it something the Roberts told you?"

For Hanover, it was all business. At least she was still working with him. There was no element of anger or consequences to be dealt with for his actions. Just a, *let's get back on track*, kind of attitude. He respected that, but he wanted to respond in a clear manner so they could remain on the same page from here on out.

"Hanover, I'm not a rogue cop. I don't think I can, nor do I want to do this alone. You have to understand my position. When Sam traded himself for the Roberts, in my opinion, that was heroic. But you guys didn't know what was going on. The same thing happened four years ago. Sam was trailing Sarah's kidnapper, and you guys didn't know. Listen, Hanover, Sam is a friend. I admire his decision and would not have tried to talk him out of it, but we should've *known*. Someone should have known."

He stopped and waited. He had implied she was to blame for the mistakes in this case and the one she bungled four years ago.

A truck stop came up on the right. He put on his blinker and pulled over. He needed more toothpicks to calm his nerves.

Maybe they'll have flavored ones.

"Parkman, look, four years ago, Sam was ordered off the

case. He was told to relinquish everything he had to us and to leave it alone. He didn't. If he had, maybe we would've been trailing the suspects, not Sam. The only reason he wasn't charged for obstruction of justice was because of what he went through trying to save Sarah's life."

Parkman heard her pull the phone away from her ear to address someone and order something checked.

"Sorry about that," Hanover said. "With Sam, he has always done things on his own. This trade he did today was a Lone Ranger stunt. How can I work with him or even protect him when he does that sort of thing? All I can do is rely on people like you because you can help, Parkman. Don't alienate us. I've got nothing to go on. Right now, I need you."

He watched the traffic on the small two-lane highway. She was right.

"Okay, but I'm in until everything is over. When Sarah is home, and all the bad guys are dead or in jail, we part ways. Deal?"

"Deal," Hanover said without hesitation.

"The Roberts described the ride out to where they were held as at least an hour without any sharp turns. This led me to believe that they were being held outside the city. I jumped on the closest highway, Route 9, and here I am, mindlessly driving around looking for what, I don't know."

"Okay, let me call the local cops in that area and see if there have been any disturbances within the last twenty-four hours. If we have Sam and Sarah out there somewhere, I'm sure they're going to fight their way out of this. I'll call you back as soon as I have something."

"Okay, Hanover, and thanks. We're both on the same

side, you know."

"I know, Parkman, I know."

She finished her last word with a click. The line went dead.

Parkman got out of his car and entered the truck stop.

After searching the store and asking the clerk, Parkman learned they didn't have flavored toothpicks. They didn't have any, and he was down to his last two.

Chapter 33

AFTER TRAVELING THREE MILES on the back road, Sarah found a driveway that meandered away into a patch of trees. She slowed and took the turn. She could be driving into gunfire if this gravel road led to the compound. The only advantage she had was the SUV—they'd see it as one of theirs and not notice anything strange until it was too late.

The sun came at the SUV at an angle, creating a glare on her right side. Sunglasses would have offered relief, but she hadn't taken the time to search the vehicle, nor was she about to now.

There was a part of her still trying to reconcile itself with having to kill people. Overall, she felt pretty good, though, which scared her. She was afraid that, if killing left no discernible mark on her, she would have lost the humane part of herself.

She realized how lucky she was. A bullet could have come out of the gun back in the interrogation room. Thinking about the interrogation room reminded her that it was only yesterday, even if it felt like weeks ago. So much had happened in that time.

She was still human enough to know that these people didn't deserve to live. They'd have been hung for their crimes a hundred years ago. Society had gotten softer while their criminals got harder.

Continuing up the driveway as it wound deeper into the forest, she realized it was probably a road but couldn't tell which yet. Turning around, a final bend brought her to the front yard of a house.

So it's a driveway.

Sarah stopped the SUV and stared at the curtained windows. Children's toys were scattered across the front lawn. A small homemade fort had been built beside a swinging tire near a large oak tree.

The house did not look like that of a ripped-shirted compound member. Could it be a red herring? Would they offer up such decoys as kids' toys to avert a more in-depth inspection by authorities?

Sarah had to be sure. She let her foot off the brake and eased forward, the tires crunching gravel. The driveway led along the side of the house toward the backyard. More children's toys littered the yard, together with normal backyard items—a barbecue beside a raised deck and lawn chairs where the owners could sit and watch the evening sun go down.

Sure now that this house had nothing to do with the compound where she had been held, Sarah did a three-point turn and eased up past the house again. As she was about to accelerate by the front lawn and down the driveway, she slammed on the brakes and turned around to see the curtains in the bay window coming to a stop.

Whoever was inside the house had looked out to watch the vehicle that had checked out their property.

As it should be.

She released the brake and moved forward again, got clear of the house, and gunned it for the road.

The compound couldn't be far. When she escaped, the walk that morning took no longer than an hour which she figured to be about five or so miles.

She would find it.

And when she did, she had no idea how to break Esmerelda and Dolan out.

All she knew was she had to.

Chapter 34

SAM HOBBLED UP THE small hallway. His leg wound needed the tourniquet retied. He briefly considered redoing the tourniquet to allow better blood flow to the healthy part of his leg but didn't want to waste time or pass out in the process.

He got to the front door and peered out through the small window. There was no one around—the place appeared deserted. Sweat covered his gun hand. With his left hand, blood still on it, he gripped the door handle and eased it in a full turn.

It didn't make a sound. A moment later, he was outside. He scouted the entire field before him, but it was barren, except for the small buildings that looked like extra-large outhouses lined up in two rows, side-by-side. Trees surrounded the rear of the buildings. From where he stood, the doors of the sheds were all sitting open.

Something wasn't right. It was too quiet. Not a single vehicle was in sight, nor any of the hostiles.

The rush of what had happened back in the room was wearing off. The loss of blood didn't help. If he didn't get to a phone soon, he could be in serious trouble out here by himself.

He leaned against the building, weight on his shoulder, and edged along the wall toward the large hangar adjacent to it.

The sun's warmth beat at the cold, clammy feeling threatening to overcome him. He found it funny how he could feel so cold but sweat so much.

Five feet from the hangar door, a wave of dizziness enveloped him. He used the wall of the hangar to keep him upright. He shut his eyes and breathed deeply, trying to remain calm.

"I see you have dispatched my colleague."

He started and jumped off the wall. The dizziness returned as he swiveled his head, looking for the voice's owner. He steadied himself on his good leg, waiting for a bullet. Was he hearing things, or did someone actually speak?

Befuddled, he moved, his leg warning him of imminent collapse. The hangar door was within reach. He saw that the glass had been lifted, and the screen was open. Whoever had spoken a moment before was inside the hangar, talking through the screen.

Heroics weren't his thing. He was the cop who always called for backup. He knew it and was okay with that fact. In order to continue to protect and serve, he'd tried his best to go by the book. One of the rare times he'd gone off the rails was four years ago, and he'd almost died.

But this time was different.

With an over-inflated sense of justice, Sam ripped open

the screen door and charged into the hangar with his remaining strength. In his mind, he recanted two words: *for Sarah.*

Once inside, he lost his balance and fell hard, the concrete floor unforgiving. He was out of options. He brought the gun up to aim at any potential targets.

"That won't be necessary," the voice said. "You're wounded. There's no fight left in you. Let it go, just let it go."

Looking down the hangar sideways, he saw the speaker was the guy with the weird glasses who had first met him when he arrived.

There was a small Cessna in the hangar and one black SUV. It was difficult to tell, but Sam thought he could see at least two heads in the back seat of the SUV. Venturing a guess, he figured it was Esmerelda and Dolan.

He looked back at the creep, who had a gun trained on him.

"Drop your weapon," Glasses said, his mouth twisted in a sly smile.

The guy's trigger finger moved. He wasn't going to wait. He was going to shoot regardless. At this range, the more competent of the two was the man standing.

With probably a few seconds left, Sam lowered his weapon to the concrete floor and said, "Where are the girls?"

"The girls?" Glasses sounded surprised.

"Yeah, the girls. Where are they? Have you already shipped them to your new *recreational* club?"

"Oh, you needn't mind yourself with the welfare of the nubiles. Everything is being taken care of. I think what should be important to you right now is your own safety.

Move the gun away from your person."

Sam pushed the weapon away. It rattled along the concrete floor a few feet from him. He dropped his head to the floor, defeated. Only God could step in now. Sam had been trained to enter and clear a room. There was no death wish here. Ultimately, he blamed it on delirium, exhaustion, and a sense of heroism.

"What were you hoping to achieve in the state you're in, hmm?" Glasses asked.

"Just tell me about your captives. Tell me about your captives if you're going to kill me anyway. Let me die with the knowledge so I won't die for nothing."

"Demanding. Even as you bite the bullet, demanding. Hmm, okay, let's make a trade. You will save me some time if you tell me what happened in the room with my interrogator. Tell me, and I will tell you what you want."

"Your man was weak and lazy. No one patted me down. I came here with a knife. I used it to slice open your interrogator's throat."

Glasses stepped back and looked at the SUV. He dropped his gun in his pants.

"The captives are gone. They're on their way to our new community, where they will join a batch of elite customers, and business will continue as usual. Now that Sarah Roberts is dead, I will have to milk every bit of psychic ability out of these two. Otherwise, Mr. Johnson, I will be leaving you here alive. You probably won't make the night, and since our establishment is so well hidden, you won't be found for quite some time. I don't believe in allowing my enemy the pleasure of a quick death."

Glasses started to walk away, but Sam stopped him with

his bellow.

"Wait!" Then, after collecting himself, he continued, "Sarah Roberts is dead?"

He could tell that Glasses was enjoying this as he turned back to Sam. Then he realized that Glasses wouldn't leave him alive after all. This game was a rhetoric that Glasses enjoyed. It was written all over his face.

"Oh, I was sure you would've heard. Sarah escaped and made it to our rest house about five miles from here. She burned down with the house. Such a promising girl. From what I've heard, we could've done great things with her. But alas, she isn't with us anymore."

"I wouldn't be too sure about that," Sam mumbled.

"I'm sorry. Come again?"

"I said I wouldn't be too sure about that. Sarah is resilient. I've seen her escape from harder things than a fire. You might want to get some confirmation."

"Oh, but I did," Glasses said as he raised his finger high. "I was contacted by my men, who were ordered to burn the house down. They confirmed she was on the top floor. The last contact wasn't too long ago."

"I still think you're wrong," Sam said as his voice weakened. He rested his head on the concrete and closed his eyes. Maybe the end would be welcoming.

Without opening his eyes, he detected movement close to him. Then he heard the sound of the hammer clicking into place. The smell of an oily metal substance was close to his face.

Then, as he anticipated a bullet, all hell broke loose from the area of the SUV.

Chapter 35

Parkman's cell phone rang. He had been watching the road from the truck stop parking lot, gnawing on one of his last toothpicks. When he saw it was Hanover on call display, he answered.

"What do you have?" he asked.

"Probably nothing, but the only serious call in the last twenty-four hours was a house fire off Route 9. What piqued my interest was the area. It's remote and perfect for the suspects to operate in. Also, no one called in the fire until a neighbor saw the smoke. Oh wait, I'm getting another call."

Parkman turned his car on and waited. Whichever way this fire was, he needed to know to get there and look around.

"Parkman, where are you right now?" Hanover came back on with an urgency to her voice.

"In a truck stop. It's called Mackie's Truck and Tow. It has a little restaurant, too."

"Okay, one sec," Hanover said and paused, then a moment later, "good, I see where you are on the map. Leave now and head two miles east. You'll come to a side road. Turn right and drive for half a mile."

Parkman put the car in gear and raced out of the parking lot, squealing his tires. He hit the highway and brought the cruiser up to eighty before asking, "What am I looking for?"

"There's a parallel road to Route 9 called Martin Road. The house fire is on Martin Road. The volunteer Fire Department is still trying to get the fire under control, but they found two bodies. One was in the pool in the backyard with bruising around his neck, a belt floating in the pool with him. The other was shot in the throat in the front yard. There has to be a connection. But I want you to go to a house about two miles from the fire."

"Why there?"

"When I was on the phone with the fire department dispatcher a moment ago, one of my people intercepted a 911 call from a woman who said someone was prowling her yard."

"I don't understand," Parkman said. "Why do you want me to go to a prowler call?"

"Because the woman said it was a black SUV, and the plate number matches one of the plates stolen from the teacher's neighborhood. With two dead guys at the fire and an SUV at this woman's house, you're the closest officer to that SUV. Keep your eyes peeled because the call came in four minutes ago. You may come upon this SUV. I gotta go, but call me as soon as you have something."

The phone went dead just as Parkman saw the sign for Martin Road. He couldn't remember which way she said to turn. Hanover didn't confirm the woman's address with him. Maybe that's why things go south for Special Agent Jill

Hanover because she mishandles information.

He took a guess, turned right, and raced along the dirt road. In under a minute, he saw smoke in the distance. That meant he was close to the house with the prowler … or it was two miles on the other side of the fire.

He looked for a driveway. Moments later, he spotted one and turned up it. The road was long and winding. The siren and lights came on as he flicked the switches. Out here, in an unmarked cruiser, he didn't want anyone to misconstrue who he was. Also, he had no backup, so he needed to come in strong if he was literally walking into a fight. He reminded himself that these guys were cop killers.

A house came into view. He flipped off the sirens but left the lights on. Just as he stopped out front, a woman in her twenties opened the front door of the house.

Parkman got out, did a quick scan of the area, and stepped toward her.

"Ma'am, did you call in a suspicious vehicle prowling around your premises?"

"Yes, I did. They drove up the driveway, stopped, and then drove around to the back, where the driver turned back around and left. It was odd, so I called it in. It was like they were checking the place out."

"Can you tell me if they went left or right when they exited your property?"

"I can't see the road from here, so no, but I can tell you they probably turned right."

"How would you know that?" Parkman asked as he glanced over his shoulder. Martin Road was lost to the trees. There was no way to see the road from the house.

"Because if you go left, it's a dead end about three miles

down. The only house down that way is the Renfeld place. I can see the smoke from here. Going right will take you three miles to the old, abandoned airport, and I …"

Parkman didn't hear the rest as he dropped back into his car. An abandoned airport was the perfect place to stash vehicles and people, especially if they had an airplane hangar there.

At the end of the driveway, Parkman turned right and raced down Martin Road away from the house fire. He passed the road back to Route 9 and continued on, hoping to catch a much-needed break in the case.

The lights still flashed, but he kept the siren off. Up a small rise, down another, a slight turn to the right, and then he hit his brakes. A black SUV was parked on the side of Martin Road. The brake lights were lit, telling Parkman the vehicle was occupied. He turned off his lights and eased up to about twenty feet from the rear of the SUV. It was a black Chevy Tahoe with tinted windows.

He speed-dialed Hanover and got her voicemail. He told her where he was and that he would be approaching the Tahoe.

With his gun on safety, he looked in each mirror to ensure this wasn't some kind of trap and stepped from his car. The open car door gave him a meager amount of shelter. He held the gun away from him, both hands on the barrel.

"Hey!" he yelled. "Step out of the vehicle slowly. Open the doors and come out with your hands where I can see them."

He detected movement in the front seat of the Tahoe. Through the darkened windows, he could barely discern someone sitting there. The back windows were tinted too much to see through.

The front door popped open an inch.

"Don't shoot. I'm coming out."

A woman's voice.

"Just make sure your hands are where I can see them," Parkman shouted. He stole a glance behind him. They were alone out here on Martin Road.

The driver's side door opened, and a young pair of female legs in track pants swung out.

Sarah Roberts.

"Take it easy, Parkman. It isn't what it looks like."

"Is anyone else in the vehicle with you?" he asked.

"No one," she said as she hopped out. "I'm alone."

Parkman lowered his weapon and stepped out from behind his car door. He hurried over to the SUV and peeked inside. The Tahoe was empty.

He holstered his weapon.

"What the hell happened to you? Whose clothes are you wearing, and why do you look like you were swimming?"

Sarah lowered her hands. "It's a long story. One that I can tell you as soon as we get everyone safe. I suspect the people you're looking for are down this road."

"Tell me what you can," Parkman said as he walked back to his cruiser. "I have to call this in while you talk. Oh, and were you the prowler call we got from a house a few miles up the road? You know, the one with a long winding driveway?"

"Yes. I was looking down each entrance on this road to see which one they were at. I knew it was within five miles. But we're running out of time. We can't wait for backup. You're it. You and me. I'm going in. I hope you're coming, too."

"Sarah, wait one minute. Let me call this in first."

Sarah walked back to the Tahoe. He watched her hop into the driver's seat while he raised Hanover on the phone. This time he got her. He explained where he was and that he had Sarah, then he was off the phone.

Parkman headed back over to the Tahoe. Sarah started talking.

"I was taken with Esmerelda. I know they have Dolan and my parents—"

"Correction. They *had* your parents."

"What?"

"Your parents are safe. Earlier today, they were given up in exchange for Sam Johnson. They have Sam instead."

"I don't know how happy I should be about that. What a shock. I think my parents are being tortured, and then I hear they're safe, but a friend like Sam is now in their midst. How crazy everything can get when …"

"Sarah, what happened to your arm?"

"I was shot twice. Once in the arm and once in the leg, but the bullets just grazed me. Listen, that's not important. It may be important tomorrow, but not today. Today, I'm going there to kill as many of these guys as possible. Are you coming?"

"Sure, but tell me more on the way," Parkman said.

They jumped in the Tahoe, Sarah driving.

"We'll use this. They won't know we're not with them until it's too late." She paused and looked at him. "How did you find me?"

"Your parents said it was about an hour's drive from town. I started driving. After an hour, I called in to see what emergency calls had been made in this area over the last day or so. A suspicious vehicle was seen at a house a little ways back. The woman called it in and gave us the plate of this vehicle. It matched the plate number we knew was on this particular gang's vehicles. Also, the fire department responded to a house fire. They found two dead men on the property." He glanced at her. "One was strangled in a pool—that's why you're wet, isn't it? One was shot in the throat. Know anything about that?"

Sarah looked at him. "They planned to kill me. I had no choice."

"Sarah, after all these years, I'm the *only* cop who trusts you. How did you get away?"

They came to a bend in the road. It was more of a road than a driveway. It was wide enough to be a two-lane highway at this point, which made sense to him if it was the old airport access road.

"I escaped from this compound and walked five miles until I came upon a house. It was empty, and I needed to call for help but also get cleaned up. I got in through a back window. Some of the men from this compound drove up in these large SUVs, and I had to hide in the attic. The next thing I know, the place is on fire. The two guys found dead were the last two to leave, but they saw me and wanted to wait to make sure I was dead. I grabbed a belt from a closet upstairs, jumped out the back window into the pool, and strangled the first guy. I took his gun and shot the second one. And now, here I am going in to get the rest. This stops here. Right now. No one survives, or they live to be able to do it all again."

Parkman stared at her with admiration and respect.

Up ahead, a line of small buildings came into view.

"Those are the jail cells they kept us in. Behind them is a large building where they interrogate and torture."

Parkman was worried they'd drive in too far. "Stop here and let me out. I'll snake along behind these buildings. The doors are all open. They look empty. If anyone is still here, they'll be in the hangar."

Sarah stopped, and Parkman jumped out. He turned to her. "Watch your back."

Sarah hit the gas and pulled away so fast that the door slammed shut on its own.

Alone, Parkman checked inside a few buildings and started for the hangar. Sarah had parked to the far right of the little barn-like building. She put the driver's side door by the tree line to have shelter when she exited the vehicle.

The only sound was the soft wind. The place had a deserted feel to it. He didn't want to admit it to himself, but he felt they were too late.

Sarah motioned to him that she was going to the back of the hangar. He nodded and showed her that he was entering through the front.

If there were still hostiles in the building, he wanted to be the first one in. He bolted for the hangar door, swung it open with one swift pull, and jumped in low, his gun ready.

Sam Johnson lay on the floor five feet away, his leg covered in blood with a strap wrapped around it like a tourniquet. His eyes were closed. If Parkman didn't see the slight movement of Sam's chest, he would've assumed Sam was dead.

Three people were near another black Tahoe. He recognized Dolan and Esmerelda right away. The third person was a man holding a large gun. The look on his face told Parkman how surprised he was to see him, too.

"Drop it!" Parkman shouted.

His eye lined up, and his finger depressed slightly. Something inside him just wanted to shoot the guy's glasses off his face.

In a blur of movement, the man dropped down and slid in behind Esmerelda. He locked a hand on her throat from behind and raised the gun to her temple.

"You drop your weapon!"

Parkman held fast for a moment. He caught his breath and eased off the trigger. Knowing Sarah was coming in behind the guy, Parkman lowered his weapon to the side.

"Throw it away," the guy yelled.

The guy would shoot as soon as the gun was a distance from him.

Where's Sarah?

She stepped out from behind the nose of the Cessna. In seconds, Sarah was behind. She bent down to rest her gun on his thigh. He jumped and looked at her.

Without saying a word, she fired her weapon and swiped at his gun with her free hand at the same moment. Parkman watched it happen from forty feet away. The guy's weapon did not discharge as it was knocked away. His leg burst in a shower of red.

Dolan grabbed Esmerelda and pulled her away so forcefully that the two of them slid a couple of feet on the floor like they were stealing second base.

A harrowing scream echoed throughout the building as the guy with the glasses grabbed at his bleeding leg.

Parkman holstered his gun and bent to check on Sam. His

pulse was weak, but he was alive.

When he looked up again, Sarah was gone. He bent to look for her feet under the SUV and the Cessna, but she had left the hangar.

He ran outside, leaving Dolan and Esmerelda alone with the screaming kidnapper. The guy was wounded, and Dolan was more than capable of dealing with him now. Parkman needed to find Sarah, but she was nowhere to be found.

The black Tahoe she drove was gone.

Sarah had disappeared.

Chapter 36

Sarah drove for at least an hour before pulling into a mall parking lot. Finding a dark corner with another SUV like hers took her five minutes. She angled the Tahoe into a spot to block the view from the mall itself. Then, wasting no time, she searched the vehicle but found no tools. The glove box only held the Tahoe's manual.

When looking under the seat, she found a quarter and used that to unscrew the license plate from a black Chevy Suburban parked on an angle taking up two spots. Careful to watch out for curious onlookers, she switched the plates and returned to the Tahoe.

Two miles away, she filled the gas tank of the Tahoe. While in the Chevron gas station, she bought a notepad, a couple of pens, two energy drinks, and an armful of snacks. Using her credit card would probably tell the authorities where she was, but she had no choice. She took out five hundred from the bank machine in the corner as a cash advance to avoid using the card again. When the police arrived at the gas station to pull the camera feeds, they would see the new plates. That meant she'd have to change the plates or the vehicle soon.

She used the restroom and got back in the SUV.

Dolan and Esmerelda were safe, and her parents were in protective custody. Now it was just her against them.

This had become personal. Her escape hadn't been that successful. She'd wanted to locate the authorities and try to bring these people down, but she had been too late. They had packed up and left, to where she had no idea, but she figured Vivian knew.

It had to do with Jack Tate somehow. Her sister had led her to him. He was the key. After being taken captive, Sarah remembered seeing no one tie Jack up, and then she hadn't seen him again. There had been no talk about him escaping. But the one thing that led her to believe he played a larger role in all this was the ripped shirts of her captors. It had to be some kind of code or symbol for their group.

If that were the case, then Vivian had some explaining to do. Why hadn't Vivian warned her? Why allow her to be dragged down into this and nearly killed? For what purpose? How could she save people if she'd been badly wounded or killed? Unless Vivian wasn't privy to that information on the Other Side. Could she know exactly what would happen and how everything would turn out? Or how Sarah would react in every situation?

What about free will? What if Sarah chose something different? How would Vivian get her results, then?

There were too many questions with no simple answers.

Sarah drove on into the afternoon with no destination in mind. She had a credit card with a few thousand still available on it but couldn't use it. Five hundred in cash and a full tank of gas in a stolen vehicle with stolen plates. Half the state police and the FBI would be on her tail soon while she hunted down prey that remained elusive.

How many people had been held in that compound back at the hangar? Where were they now? Could this be her last job as an automatic writer?

She hadn't thought of herself as expendable before. Maybe this was it. The police would be able to tell that it was Sarah who killed the two men at the house fire. She even admitted it to Parkman, a cop, earlier today. It would take months to deal with all that had happened in the past several days.

Time was a luxury Sarah did not have.

Somewhere out there, a man named Jack Tate was connected to the murder of her sister.

One thing she was pretty sure of was that he was part of this larger, murderous group.

A group that Sarah intended to bring down before she stopped to fill in paperwork for the authorities.

Chapter 37

ARMOND TRIED THE CELL number again. It went directly to voicemail.

"Fuck! Where is everybody? I can't get through. Are they dead, or have they been arrested?"

Jeffries leaned back and turned around in the front passenger seat. "Armond, we are safely away. We have a large head start. Once we are secure in the new compound and our vehicles are shielded, we can take care of the people who caused this."

Armond glared at him. "That is precisely the problem. I only have four guards now. We have eighteen girls on that bus. You know how this is done. There are always two with me and two with the girls."

"I understand," Jeffries said, nodding. He looked at his watch. "We will be in Colorado in six hours. Surely some of Tom's security could stand in while Kent and I take care of Sarah Roberts. She's just a girl. It will be our pleasure."

Armond shook his head. "No, too risky. I have something

else in mind for Sarah. Just get us to Colorado."

Armond looked down at his cell phone and dialed Tom Jacobs's private line. Tom answered on the fourth ring, slightly out of breath.

"Tom, it's Armond. What's happening there?"

"We are preparing for your arrival. The short notice has my select few working extra hard to accommodate the number of people you bring with you."

"Have you prepared secured sleeping arrangements for the girls and my men?"

"Yes. I have decided to put the girls on the temple's top floor. That's where they will be the most secure. We already have beds up there for other church business, so I've had my men carry up the rest to accommodate your needs."

"Good. There are a few other things I'm going to need," Armond said as he stared out the tinted window of the Tahoe.

The American countryside raced by. At times he wondered if he was delusional or, worse, psychopathic. But a madman never doubted his sanity. He felt great, in power and control. Hearing that Sarah was alive and his two good men were left for dead at the resting house nearly drove him over the edge. He only hoped Dolan and Esmerelda were dead now. Since he'd lost contact with the remaining crew member at the hangar, he could only assume the worst.

"I need you to call that local marshal, the believer, and ask him to give you a location on one of my SUVs." Armond read the vehicle identification number to Tom. "I need him to search for it as privately as he can using OnStar or the security system tracker or whatever he can, but I need it found as soon as humanly possible. Can you do this?"

"Yes, I can. It will be handled. I'll contact you as soon as he gets an ID on its location."

"We are about six hours' drive away. You will be ready for us, yes?"

"Of course."

Armond hit the end button and turned to look back out the window. He marveled at how simple life was for the people in the cars that raced by going the other way. These businessmen and families he saw in their Cadillacs and minivans had no idea that the tour bus ahead of Armond carried kidnapped girls to please men like the ones driving their families to Disney Land. How could they know? The tour bus had blacked-out windows and was labeled with church insignia. Armond had always been friendly with the fundamental Mormons, who tended to congregate in secured compounds away from the general public. They believed, in certain excommunicated groups, that it was right to arrange marriages for twelve- and fourteen-year-olds. Armond had left the Texas compound just a few days before the early April 2008 raids on Warren Jeffs's outfit.

He didn't believe in their doctrines. But these people gave him a place to hide when he needed one.

He scrolled through the phone numbers in his cell, located the one he wanted, and hit send.

It was answered instantly.

"I need a job handled," Armond said.

"Go on."

"There's a girl that needs to be dealt with. Her name is Sarah Roberts. I don't know where she is, but I may know within the hour. Can you do this?"

"Yes. Call me back when you know where she is."

"There's something you should know," Armond added.

He couldn't allow any more mistakes with Sarah. She appeared all too capable. "This girl is quite good. I have to warn you to be careful. She is extremely professional and has been trained well."

"I understand. I will be prepared and waiting to move out at your call. This may cost you more than the normal amount."

"Do the job well, and I will pay you accordingly."

Armond ended the call and tilted his head back on the seat. The man he had called, an ex-marine, had come back from his tour of duty with Post Traumatic Stress Disorder and had turned into one of the best hit men Armond had ever used. To date, he tried to remember how many hits he'd used him on and stopped counting around twelve. Americans had no idea what the real statistics were. How many people go missing every year? How many were fed to pigs at pig farms? How many were dropped in the Everglades with two broken legs and two broken arms, never to be heard from again as the alligators got fatter?

Thanks to people like Elson, anyone who crossed Armond had disappeared for good and without a trace.

Sarah Roberts would finally be taken care of the right way. The way he should've done it in the first place. The only sour note was that he wouldn't get the pleasure of doing it himself.

His phone rang. PRIVATE showed up on call display.

"Yeah."

"It's Tom. The marshal called me back. OnStar got a hit. The vehicle is traveling south on 84, going toward Salt Lake City. That vehicle could be at our compound in five to six hours. By tomorrow morning, if that's where it's headed."

"Okay, nothing to worry about. I will take care of it. Keep me posted when it stops. I've got someone meeting it. I need to hear back from you the moment it stops."

"Got it."

Armond terminated the call and dialed Elson back.

"She's traveling on 84, heading south toward Salt Lake City. Start after it now, and I'll call you when she stops for the night."

"Anything else?"

"Do not underestimate her."

"I'm an hour's drive from Salt Lake City. Call me back when you have more. I'll leave now."

Chapter 38

Sarah fingered the piece of paper beside her.

Fredonia, Arizona.

Every mile was a blessing. In a stolen SUV with a trail of dead cops and dead goons, every cop in the state was looking for her.

The only reason she got away was because of Parkman. No other cop knew her as he did. No other cop would've trusted her as he did.

She flipped on the radio and scanned stations to see if she could catch anything on the news.

There was no way she was going to try to make it to Fredonia in this vehicle. She would have to change cars somewhere in Salt Lake City. She had no idea how yet; she just knew she had to. Maybe a classified ad would be all she needed. Some twenty-year-olds might want to trade for the SUV. She could only hope, otherwise stealing a car …

She sat up straight as an idea formed.

Four years ago, Gert had taught her how to get a car that

would prove effective. In the morning, she would do it.

All she needed was a cheap motel that accepted cash and no names.

After buying the paper and pens, Sarah drove with no destination in mind. Many of the perpetrators who had orchestrated the kidnappings and murders were gone, along with whoever else they still had. She would never catch up with them, spending the next few weeks making police statements. So she had taken off. Let them figure out the whole picture first, and when she finally returned, she could fill in the blanks.

Half an hour into driving, she pulled over to urinate in bushes by the side of the road, far away from highway traffic. Her arm went numb when she got back in the driver's seat. The familiar pull from the Other Side caused her to grab the pen before passing out.

Minutes later, pen held rigid in her hand, she woke to two messages. One said *Fredonia, Arizona*, and the other said, *10:18 p.m., get a drink*.

That was it. No reason to get a drink, or what kind of drink? Was it a celebratory beverage for having stayed alive this long? Or should she walk out to the motel vending machine and purchase a drink there, provided she was sleeping in a motel and not the back seat of the Tahoe? Most of all, she wondered why?

This was the part she got so pissed off about. If Vivian was willing to take the time to channel through her for important, life-changing reasons, then why be so cryptic? Why not just spill everything she needed to know?

I'm left in the dark without a chance in hell, she thought as she started back onto the highway. She was alone, scared, and chasing murderers, and her sister wasn't helping.

A sign passed saying Salt Lake City was still forty-five miles away. She'd be on the outskirts in less than an hour.

Her adrenaline was oozing off, and her eyelids were getting heavy. She wanted a long hot bath and a warm bed.

"If something really bad was coming at 10:18 p.m. tonight, then why not write that?" she asked out loud. "I might not listen to this message, you know. Let's see what happens then."

She slammed the steering wheel, then flipped the radio stations around until she heard The Rolling Stones singing "Emotional Rescue." Leaving it on that station, Sarah sang along.

"Why?" she shouted at the windshield. "Why did so many people have to die? Actually, why do we have killers and kidnappers in this world in the first place?"

No answer came. No one spoke from the Other Side. Her arm didn't go numb. She was alone in a stolen SUV with no help from anyone, and no one knew where she was.

She drove toward a destiny not of her making but one that dragged her into the bowels of the human condition and soiled her with its dismal filth.

She drove on, knowing it was the right thing to do, knowing she had no choice.

She drove on, alone and crying.

Chapter 39

PARKMAN STARED THROUGH HIS windshield, trying to figure out why Sarah had run. It didn't bode well for her.

The FBI had shown up. Other than giving a statement, he was no longer needed here. Dolan and Esmerelda were being treated by medical personnel, and the guy Sarah shot was being tended to before his full interrogation.

So far, a threat of all the crimes perpetrated here falling solely on his plate, including all the murders, got the guy talking. He had no idea where his colleagues were relocating to, but he did acknowledge that they had at least a dozen young girls in a church bus.

Armond Stuart, also known as Jack Tate, a former police officer and brother to Alex Stuart, was the head of the group. He'd been doing it for dozens of years.

Parkman had missed him by an hour. He called Hanover before she arrived at the hangar and asked her to see if they could get a record of Sarah's credit card and debit card purchases. Sarah wouldn't get far without money. Then he took the highway heading south toward the Mormon capital, Salt Lake City. They might be heading that way if they were in a bus trying to pass it off as a church group.

He answered his cell as it rang, moving his last toothpick to the other side of his mouth. Sometimes they got in the way, but he had no choice. He felt lost without one dangling from his lips.

"You got anything?" he asked.

"How did you know it was me?" Hanover asked.

"Guessed. Have you got anything on Sarah?"

"Her credit card paid for gas and a five-hundred-dollar cash advance at a Chevron about forty miles south of the hangar. How close are you to that area?"

"I'm coming up on it soon," Parkman said. "I'll get back to you when I have something. Call me if there are any more pings on her cards."

He hung up, pushed the cruiser harder, bringing his speed up to eighty miles an hour, and flipped the light on his dash.

Within ten minutes, a Chevron came into view. In a slew of dust, Parkman pulled in and stopped by the gas pumps.

He spit out his toothpick and headed for the store.

The door banged shut behind him when he entered. "I need to speak to the manager," he said, pulling out his badge. "I need him now. This is an emergency."

The young clerk behind the counter lost color in his face. "I'm sorry … ah, he's not here. Is there anything I can help you with?"

"A blonde girl, twenty-two years old, came through here in a black Tahoe with tinted windows roughly thirty minutes ago. She was dressed in men's clothing. Does this ring a bell?"

The clerk frowned and, in the act of trying to show he was thinking, raised a hand to his chin and frowned.

"Look," Parkman continued, "I need access to your cameras to see if she was here and to see if I can get a plate number. Can you do this for me?"

The door chimed as a woman came in to pay for her gas. She walked to the counter, edged around Parkman, and tossed a twenty at the clerk. "That's for pump three."

The clerk nodded, and the woman walked out.

"So, can you get me access to your cameras?" Parkman tried again.

"Sure, I guess. Come around the counter."

Parkman walked around and sat in the clerk's chair as he rewound the digital camera to a half hour ago. The clerk explained that the digital security system would hold a few months' memory.

In five minutes of watching and two other customers interrupting the clerk, Parkman saw what he was looking for. A black Tahoe pulled in, and Sarah Roberts got out.

"This is it. I need a pen and paper."

The clerk handed it to him. Some of the color had returned to the clerk's face.

"What's your name, kid?"

"Samuel."

"Sam, I like that name. I know a good cop named Sam. He was shot today doing something a lot of cops wouldn't do. Listen, I need gas. While I finish here, go out and gas up my cruiser. You can see it. I parked by the pumps."

"I, ah, I'm not supposed to leave the counter."

"Just go and gas up my car. I'm at the counter. What, do you think someone will steal from you when you have a cop sitting here? Oh, and can you get me some toothpicks? You guys sell toothpicks, right? I have to have toothpicks."

The clerk nodded and left. He looked pale again. Maybe that bit about Sam getting shot scared him. Parkman was just trying to make conversation. He didn't mean it to frighten the kid.

Parkman looked back at the small TV screen and pushed play. He watched as Sarah gassed up. She came onto the store's interior camera to pay for snacks. He could see two Red Bulls in her hand. She used the cash machine in the corner and then left the store. Before she sped off camera, he wrote down the Tahoe's license plate number.

The clerk showed back up and handed him a box of toothpicks.

"Thanks. I've got what I need. How much do I owe you for the gas and the toothpicks?"

"Forty-eight even," the clerk said.

Parkman nodded, paid, and thanked him before running out the door.

He called Hanover and gave her the plate number to run through the computers. It belonged to a Suburban owned by a guy who lived ten minutes from where Parkman was right now.

"That means Sarah switched the plates knowing we'd be looking for her," Parkman said.

"Things are looking worse for Sarah every minute, Parkman. Is she still the girl you know, or has she lost it?"

"I have no idea, Hanover. All I can tell you is we must bring her in to find out. Until then, I will assume she is clean, and I think you should, too. She saved my life in that airplane hangar. That guy had Esmerelda and Dolan. He would've killed us all. Without her, more people would be dead."

"Fair enough, but get her reined in. She's not a cop, and we can't have vigilantes running around."

Parkman ended the call and grabbed the new toothpicks, opening the package and tossing one in his mouth in one fluid motion.

He felt good knowing he was on Sarah's tail.

Better me than another cop who would shoot first and ask questions later.

For the umpteenth time that day, Parkman hit the gas hard, flipped his lights on, and raced after Sarah Roberts.

Chapter 40

Sarah watched for motels as soon as she could see the lights of Salt Lake City. Nothing looked secluded enough, but she was getting tired, and those two energy drinks had gone through her already. Either she found a motel soon, or she slept in the Tahoe.

She decided to try on the other side of the city, so she continued on the bypass and headed for Veteran's Memorial Highway. On the south side now, she turned off on Highland Drive and pulled into a Motel 6.

The sign out front was lit in red announcing *vacancy*. She parked near the front desk and headed in. The clerk was a young man wearing a nice blue suit jacket.

"Can I help you?" he asked.

He studied her bruised face and the men's clothes she wore. She looked at his nametag.

"Cliff," she whispered and then looked back at the door. "I'm in a little trouble. I wonder if you could help me out?"

"I'm not sure, but I could certainly try. What can I do for

you?"

Sarah looked back at the door one more time to see if anyone was listening. The clerk followed her gaze.

"My boyfriend has been cheating on me. The problem is he gets pretty violent, as you can see." She brought her hands to her face and showed him her crusted-over bullet wound on her arm. "When I found out about it, I texted him that I was going back to our place to get my stuff and move out. I figured I had time since he was at work. He got home before me and threw all my stuff in the fire pit in the back. That's why I'm wearing his clothes. Then he hit me, and I had to run. If he comes looking for me, I'm afraid he'll kill me."

"Why don't you just call the police?" Cliff asked, looking unsettled.

"Oh, no," Sarah said. "The last time I did that, I was in the hospital for weeks. Look, all you need to do is let me park my SUV in the back somewhere and rent me two rooms. One will stay empty with my name on it, and I'll sleep in the other one. I'll pay you for both, just don't tell anyone. In the morning, I'm gone from here and his life forever. That's all I'm asking. Can you do that?"

The clerk looked around the lounge as if he was afraid of the boyfriend too.

"So you'll pay for two rooms, stay the night and leave and that's all you want to do?"

"Yes, I just don't want to use a credit card."

"Okay, that's fine with me."

Cliff processed it and put her in room 104 by her name. Room 107 would remain empty but would be the one Sarah would sleep in. She moved the Tahoe to the back and walked up to 107. After using her key to unlock the door, she entered the small room with one bed. The dresser had a television on it and an open door at the back that led to the bathroom.

She grabbed the chair from the desk/dresser area and jammed it under the door handle. As she headed for the bed, she took out the papers with Vivian's prophecies and tossed them into the wastebasket. She checked her gun and applied the safety.

Intent on resting for a few minutes, Sarah flopped down on the bed, arms spread, gun by the pillow, and moaned. She couldn't find the strength to turn the lamp off by the bed. Her eyes barely functioned when she looked at the alarm clock. It read 7:32 p.m. According to her sister, she had over two and a half hours until she needed to go for a drink.

A dilemma for another time, Sarah thought as she drifted off to sleep.

Chapter 41

ELSON ACQUIRED THE FINAL address from Armond and pulled into the motel parking lot around ten in the evening. He checked that his gun and hunting knife were secure and got out of his car. The parking lot had a random assortment of vehicles. Pickup trucks, Saturns, an old Volvo, and a beat-up Chrysler littered the lot, but no black Tahoe.

Armond said it was here, so it had to be.

Elson had parked in the far corner, so if he had to leave in a hurry, he could quickly run out to his car and be gone by the back entrance.

He headed for the rear of the motel, and that was where he found the Tahoe. He checked that the doors were secure and walked around to the back of the Tahoe, away from the view of the motel. Sure that no one was watching, he dropped to the ground and slithered under the chassis. From inside his breast pocket, he pulled out a small explosive device. He set the timer for 10:18 p.m.

That would give him enough time to deal with the clerk,

find Sarah, execute her, and leave. With the SUV in ruins, the police would have little to go on.

He got up, looked around, and sauntered away from the vehicle as if he didn't have a care in the world.

The lights of the lobby were a bright contrast to the darkness outside. Even for a small lobby, the Motel 6 had extra lights in the ceiling, making the front counter look like the sun was shining through a porthole directly onto it.

Elson rang the silver bell on the counter.

A young man walked out from the back office.

"How can I help you?" he asked. "Do you need a room? We still have a few left."

"Actually, I'm looking for my sister. We're supposed to meet here. She would've checked in about two to three hours ago. Younger than me, about twenty-two years old. Her name is Sarah Roberts."

The clerk took a step back. His eyes faltered, looking down at the registry, then back up to stare at Elson.

"I'm sorry, but I can't give out information regarding the people who get rooms here. That's confidential." He set a hand on the counter in an attempt to appear firm on that point. "Although come to think of it, I don't remember anyone fitting that description."

Elson might have believed that the clerk knew nothing about Sarah if he hadn't taken that step back.

He glanced at the door. It had a thumb lock. "Okay, maybe I'll just call her on her cell phone to see where she is."

Elson stepped away from the counter. When he got to the door, he flicked the lock into place. He pulled out his Glock and turned back to the clerk. He could tell the idiot had hit some kind of alarm under the counter because he was leaning and hadn't noticed the gun yet.

With the Glock held firm at his side, he walked up to and around the counter. The clerk backed against the wall.

"Look, I'm sorry, I said I can't—"

"Tell me what room she's in. Her vehicle is in the back. I know she's here, so make it easy on yourself and tell me where she is, or you'll die, and I'll just look in the registry."

The gun found its way to the clerk's chin. His eyes widened as he looked down at the cold steel. An understanding crossed his face.

"Okay, okay, take it easy. I put her in room 104. She's in room 104. Just take it easy …"

Elson lowered the gun and stepped back. "That wasn't too hard, now was it?" He turned and looked under the counter, where he saw a panic button. "You pushed this?"

The fear on the guy's face was evident. "She said you beat her up and to not let you near her. She said you burned her clothes …"

"She says a lot, doesn't she?" Elson moved in quickly. The gun dropped into this shoulder holster as his other hand yanked the knife out in a fluid motion. The blade opened slash marks on the clerk's arms. Four quick gashes would render the clerk less effective for the time it would take to deal with Sarah.

The clerk dropped to the floor on his back, his face askew with pain and fear. Elson watched him writhe, screaming about his arms, and then he stepped out from behind the counter and headed for the door.

"Don't go anywhere. We have to have another talk when I'm done with Sarah."

He looked at his watch. 10:15 p.m. He had three minutes

left before the bomb in the Tahoe detonated.

He got to the door, unlocked it, and jogged down the line of rooms until he hit the door for 104. There wasn't any time left for subtlety.

With a quick pull on the weapon, he shot two bullets into the door handle and stepped back. He re-holstered the weapon and lunged forward, his right foot connecting with the door an inch from the splintered handle.

After a crack of protest, the motel room door burst open. Elson ran in and smacked the lights on.

The room was empty.

There's no way that little punk lied to me.

Elson ran to the back of the room, but the bathroom was empty, too.

He bolted from the room and raced back to the lobby. His gun wasn't suppressed, so no doubt someone would've heard the shots. The Tahoe would blow up this minute or the next, and now the lobby door to the Motel 6 was locked.

In frustration at how fast this job went wrong, Elson used another bullet to shoot out the door's glass. It crashed in a cascade of violent noises that he was sure others would hear over the gun.

The inside of the door had a push bar for exiting, so instead of jumping through the now glassless door, he reached in and, mindful not to touch any shards of glass, unlocked the thumb bolt.

He swung the door open, entered the lobby, and ran to the counter.

The clerk was nowhere in sight, but the registry was. He scanned the names and saw that a notation was made by Sarah's name along with room 104. The same little pen mark was ticked by room 107, but no name was on that room. It indicated the room was empty.

She must have rented two rooms and stayed in the unmarked room. Smart, but all it had succeeded in doing was stall him a few minutes. And angered him.

He exited the lobby. As he passed room 104's open door, a huge blast woke up the night behind the motel. Glass shattered, and a woman screamed from one of the rooms.

Then he saw the door to room 107 and pulled out his Glock. He would make it quick and then get the hell out.

The cops wouldn't be more than a few minutes away by now.

He shot two bullets into the door handle and ran at the door.

Chapter 42

A LOUD NOISE JOLTED her out of sleep. Did she dream it, or was there a car accident in front of the motel?

She leaned up on the bed, rubbed her eyes, and looked at the alarm clock. 10:19 p.m.

She sat up and swung her legs over the side of the bed. Vivian said to go for a drink at 10:18 p.m., and now, a minute later, she was awakened by something outside. Sarah grabbed her gun, jumped from the bed, and ran for the bathroom.

She was sure the explosion came from the back of the motel. The bathroom window was cracked. She stood on the tub's edge, unlocked the window, and slid it open carefully.

The Tahoe she had stolen was completely engulfed in flames.

They had found her.

Whoever *they* were, they were here.

She hopped off the edge of the tub, turned on the bathroom light to make it look like she was using it, splashed water in her face, and stepped back into the motel room, her gun ready. The lamp she had decided to not turn off earlier cast an ominous feel on an area that once felt safe but now had become another jail. She was trapped inside without any idea of what was going on outside.

Two shots were fired outside her door. She saw the door knob bend and parts of it shatter.

Shit.

The door buckled as something thumped into it. Whoever was on the other side was attempting to get in.

How the fuck did they find me so fast?

The only place to hide was beside the bed against the wall.

The chair she had placed under the door handle held up with the first kick. Hopefully, it gave her enough time to do what was needed.

Sarah fixed the wrinkles in the bed to make it look untouched. Next, she squeezed herself into the foot area of the desk/dresser, her gun hand placed on her knees to help steady her aim.

Another kick and the motel room door still didn't give.

She breathed in and out as fast and quietly as possible to calm her nerves. Sleep cobwebs remained, but she was ready.

For a brief moment, she chastised Vivian. How come she hadn't warned her of this attack? Or was going for a drink at 10:18 p.m. supposed to be warning enough? Life happens, and Vivian had to realize that sometimes Sarah wouldn't be able to do exactly as she was told.

The door to her motel room burst open. The sounds of the night came with it. She heard a distant siren wailing somewhere, probably on its way there.

The cold steel of the gun comforted her, but it also

reaffirmed the life she had chosen. If she had booked one room, didn't use the chair under the door knob or was a heavier sleeper, she would be dead by now. Instead, she was hiding under a desk with a fighting chance.

"I see you," the intruder said. "Come on out."

She considered it but fought the urge. If he really saw her, then he could come and get her. He had to be bluffing.

She moved the gun on an angle to visually make sure the safety was off. Funny how life hung in the balance of deeds, whether done correctly or not. It all came down to who had the surprise factor or the faster weapon.

"I said come out!" he shouted.

He stepped deeper into the room. The light coming in from the street dimmed. The amount of time he took to enter the room drove her crazy.

She saw a cowboy boot first, then a pant leg.

He had to assume she was in the bathroom. Otherwise, he wouldn't expose himself to her position. Would she be able to crawl out of her hiding spot and leave when he got to the back of the room? She wanted to walk away from this without killing him if possible. Had she listened to Vivian, the man standing in her room wouldn't be a risk.

Or should she let him go? After all, he had broken into her room to do her harm. Who else had he killed? Who would be next? Another innocent young girl? If left alive, would he try to kill Sarah again tomorrow or the day after?

He stood right in front of her now. The sirens grew louder. There wasn't much time left. He had to know that.

He stepped away from her and, in a crouched position, brought his gun around to the empty bathroom. He would probably check the open bathroom window out.

She rolled out of hiding as he stepped into the bathroom, stood, and hurried to the wall by the bed. In her rush to get into position, she almost tripped on the bedspread sticking out by the corner of the mattress. She caught herself from falling at the last second and stopped short of the wall without banging into it.

He jumped out of the bathroom, holstered his weapon, and started for the door.

Instead of killing him or letting him leave, she would maim him so he would never be able to hunt innocent girls again.

With the precision she'd learned at a firing range, she aimed at the back of his moving right knee and squeezed the trigger gently.

As soon as her weapon spit out a bullet, the man's jeans burst open directly in front of the knee where the bullet exited. He shouted and fell to the motel room floor.

Surprisingly, in mid-fall, he was already reaching for his weapon. She aimed for his gun arm and fired.

The carpet beside him puffed up where the bullet smacked it.

She'd missed.

His weapon was out now. She fired but missed again. It wasn't her skill faltering as much as her nerves thwarting her.

She jumped over the edge of the bed and closed the five-foot gap to stand over him, firing into his right arm before his weapon was properly aimed.

Another scream from him, and his gun dropped out of his hand as she shot precisely into his elbow.

Screeching tires echoed throughout the room as police cars pulled up to the motel's lobby.

There was no fear on his face, only pain. Anger and hatred too. It allowed her to finish what she had started.

With the grace of an expert, Sarah brought her weapon down in line with his other knee and said, "Give me your car keys, or you will never walk again."

"Fuck you," he said and turned from her to spit onto the carpet.

She fired point blank into the top of his other kneecap, on an angle that went down through it and into the femur. She did this with a sense of calm, a sense of peace, knowing that, in the end, she had saved lives today by making this man a cripple. That was his sentence to serve for the crimes he had committed.

No jury would agree but fuck them.

She shoved her gun in the back of her pants and bent to fish in his pockets as he thrashed around on the floor. The car keys were easy to find. She pulled them out and was surprised at the fight left in him.

His only good limb, the left arm, had come up with a hunting knife. The lazy jab for her missed by a foot. She stood and, with one swift movement, kicked the knife out of his hand.

Even as he bled and his body went into shock, he still had a fight in him. Left alive, he would be tormented by the anger that ate at him on the inside.

She ran to the door and looked out. Three cruisers sat in front of the motel office. Maybe the guy in her room had hurt or killed the clerk. She hoped he wasn't dead, but it explained why the cops weren't going door to door yet.

She left the room and started toward the back of the motel. The keys had no markings on them to tell her what kind of car she was looking for, but they had a fob.

She repeatedly pushed the lock and unlock buttons until, at the back corner beside the exit ramp, a Nissan Altima's lights flicked on.

In under two minutes, Sarah was in the Nissan and heading south toward Fredonia.

Chapter 43

WHAT A MESS. IT sure made the cops look inept. They always seem to be doing the cleanup. The criminals had no work ethic. They did what they wanted, whenever they wanted, with no rules governing them. No law books to study and no one to answer to but themselves, whereas Parkman had a boss. Special Agent Jill Hanover had a boss. They all had a job to do, and each one of them had to keep within the rules of that job.

His cell phone rang, cutting off his thoughts.

"Hello. Parkman here."

"I'm coming down there to get a handle on everything."

"Hanover, there's no handle to get. Sarah's gone, and we have no idea where to. The Tahoe is destroyed, and the guy that attacked her in her room is undergoing emergency surgery at a hospital in Salt Lake City, so I can't talk to him until at least the morning, and then we all know he'll lawyer up. The motel clerk is being treated for slash wounds to his arms. All he said was that Sarah was on the run from an abusive boyfriend."

"I'm coming anyway. Gather anything you can from any of the other motel guests. Did they see Sarah? Did they witness …"

"I know how to do my job, Hanover. I'll find out whatever I can before you get here."

Parkman stepped out of room 107 and stared up at the darkened sky.

"Why do you sound dejected?" Hanover asked. "Is there something you haven't told me, Parkman?"

"I'm pissed off. I'm sick and tired of showing up after the fact. I'm sick of cleaning up crime scenes and looking for clues to maybe, one day, find the bad guys. Sarah is out there alone, and all we're doing for support is trying to follow her, and for what? What exactly are we doing?"

"Our jobs," Hanover said. "That's what the police do. Come on, Parkman, you know how this works. How are we supposed to know where to go and who to arrest without evidence and proof? Just …" she paused.

"Just what?"

"Just don't do anything until I get there. Ask around and see what you can find out."

"Hanover, it's almost three in the morning. This all went down over four hours ago. Everyone is asleep."

"I'm on my way," she said and disconnected.

Parkman dropped his phone back in his breast pocket and looked toward the front desk. One cruiser was still parked out front. He turned around and stared at Sarah's room.

"What happened here? Where have you gone?" he asked the empty room.

After examining the room thoroughly, Parkman had

already deduced most of what had happened. Sarah had hidden somewhere, either behind the bed or in the foot space of the desk/dresser, and made it look like she was in the bathroom. There were no signs of water in the sink or shower, though. Then, as the guy was about to leave, she shot out one knee. Parkman could see where she might have missed a couple of shots, but hitting his arm would have been difficult in this small room.

He walked the scene out again and stood where Sarah would've stood as she shot one more bullet into the guy's other leg from the front.

Down on bended knee, Parkman scanned the area beside the bed but couldn't tell if Sarah had crouched there. Wouldn't the intruder have seen her before he got to the bathroom? Maybe she hadn't hidden beside the bed. Maybe she had used the foot space on the desk.

He hobbled over on his knees and tried to crawl in, knowing Sarah was much smaller than he was.

It would work. She could fit in there and stay relatively hidden unless the guy looked directly down and bent in a little.

He crawled back out and pulled the worn toothpick he was munching on out of his mouth. When he turned to throw it in the garbage, he saw a crumpled-up piece of paper in the can.

Why didn't he think to look in the wastebasket before? Why hadn't the local cops?

He grabbed the paper, opened it, and instantly recognized Sarah's handwriting, as he'd seen it so many times over the years.

Fredonia, Arizona. 10:18 p.m., get a drink.

"That's it," he said aloud.

It was right after ten when the clerk had said the intruder had shown up. That meant these messages were from Vivian. Why wasn't Sarah out of the room at 10:18 p.m. then? Did she plan on torturing the guy? Did she lie in wait?

That kind of reasoning led him down a path he didn't want to go. But the bed didn't look slept in. He'd already examined room 104. It was clear that Sarah didn't even go into that room.

So why didn't she do what Vivian told her to and leave the room at 10:18 p.m.? Unless she did but came back to surprise the intruder.

This didn't look good for Sarah. Before anyone else got to her, he needed to find her and sort everything out.

And he figured he would find Sarah in Fredonia, Arizona.

He pulled out his cell phone and dialed Hanover. Then, before the first ring, he canceled the call.

No, this time, it'll be on my terms.

Hanover could get to the motel and ask the tenants all the questions she wanted. She and her *special agents* could do the cleanup.

Parkman was going after Sarah. He wouldn't answer his cell phone either. Let them think his battery had died.

He stepped out of room 107 and realized he was still holding his toothpick. He flipped his wrist, tossing it to the ground.

Minutes later, he was in his cruiser, heading toward Fredonia, a new toothpick swishing back and forth, calming his nerves.

Chapter 44

SARAH PULLED OVER ON the outskirts of Fredonia around four in the morning at a truck stop and slept for two hours. She woke feeling like she could sleep another day.

Her wounds were healing well. The bruise on her face had turned a jaundiced yellow. The bullet wounds were covered over well with no signs of infection.

She eased out of the cramped driver's seat and stood beside the car to stretch. The sun was rising in the east, and hell was waiting in the south.

Sometimes a good stretch wasn't enough. Her injured arm felt stiffer. She shut the car door and walked over to the entrance of the all-night truck stop. Inside, two men were eating breakfast, and one guy bought a coffee. Other than that, the place was empty.

After using the toilet, she washed her face with cold water. Now awake and cognizant, she was ready to do what she came to do.

Voices from the restaurant wafted in through the

bathroom door. She stepped out and almost walked right into a state trooper.

"Excuse me, I'm sorry," she said and moved around him, careful to keep her head down in case her picture had been circulated.

"Ma'am?"

Sarah stopped.

"Ma'am, are you okay? Let me take a look at your face?"

Sarah lifted her head and looked into the intense blue eyes of a cop in his mid-twenties.

"I'm fine … basketball accident. My girlfriends and I get a little rough during twenty-one."

He stared at her a moment longer and then offered her an out. "Are you sure?"

Sarah nodded and turned to leave. He let her go.

The cop would be perfect. She was ready to change cars, and, as Gert taught her four years ago, a cop car was the best for what she had in mind.

She climbed into the driver's seat of the Nissan and waited for the cop to get back in his car.

The Nissan had a pad of paper attached to a plastic sticky thing on the dash with handwriting on it. When she pulled it off the dash, she realized why her arm was so cramped. She must have written this note when asleep. There were three pages of text.

Why had Vivian waited this long to explain everything to her?

As she read, she kept glancing at her mirrors to ensure she didn't miss the cop.

Alex Stuart wasn't Armond Stuart's son, the note said. They were brothers. This had nothing to do with Armond's talk of voodoo and everything to do with human smuggling. It always had been, only on a smaller scale years ago. She learned that Jake Tate, as she suspected, was Armond. All that time, she had the leader of this smuggling ring in her possession, and he fooled her, too.

She checked the mirrors, but the state trooper was still inside.

She continued with the notes, but all that was left was an address and a warning. The warning said that the address was for the police. Sarah was supposed to hand it over to the police and let them deal with Armond. He had the victims in some kind of fundamentalist Mormon compound where he hid with a few mercenaries. Vivian called it *FLDS*.

I'm just supposed to hand this information over to the police after all I've gone through?

"Then why do this at all?" she asked out loud. "If you can hear me, Vivian, I want an answer. Why did you send me after him in the first place? Why did you lie and let me think those men at his house were going to kill him? Why not just write it all out in the first place and let me hand that over to the police then, huh? Why?"

Sarah smacked the passenger seat beside her with the back of her hand.

"Is it not enough that I almost died? They kidnapped our parents. Why did that have to happen? Is this some kind of joke for you? Is that what I *am* to you, a fucking joke? Well, Vivian, I will not just hand this over to the police. I have the address of this FLDS compound. I will break down its doors and make those responsible pay for what they did. Do you hear me?"

She caught a glimpse of her tear-streaked face in the

mirror. The hurt, the anger, and the feelings of being used overwhelmed her. It was okay to break down. It felt good to let it out. She held on to things too much. Actually, she had a right to be pissed off, too.

"I agreed to respond to your messages because of how it made me feel. I love helping others. I know there are risks. I'm willing to take them on most days. But when you intentionally lead me into harm's way, I need to know why, or I won't be able to trust you. Do you hear me?" Sarah raised a fist. "No, I will not give this to the police. I will finish it on my own. Or was that your plan? Taunt me and goad me into choosing my own path. Is that why you also warned me that it's too dangerous for me alone? What, am I not good enough to deal with it? If this kills me, then we'll be together. Is that what you want? I assure you, when I come to your side, I'm going to fucking smack you for this." She stopped and looked down at the written warning. *Attempt on your own at great personal risk. Don't do it. The chances of survival are slim.* "We'll see about that."

Sarah tossed the papers on the passenger seat and wiped her face with both hands. A shudder and then a deep breath helped to collect herself.

She looked in the mirror to see if the state trooper's vehicle was still there.

It was gone.

She started the Nissan and squealed out to the highway.

A minivan passed her, heading south. A Subaru raced by going north. She had no way of knowing which way he went. She chose south. The state trooper was an Arizona trooper as far as she could remember. He'd be patrolling the highway and not heading toward Utah.

There was no way for her to establish how far ahead he was, only that he would probably be doing the speed limit or thereabouts. As the Nissan raced to eighty miles an hour, she hoped he hadn't had to respond to a call.

Passing car after car, Sarah chased the trooper, careful not to lose control. Ten minutes later, she saw him ahead and whispered a soft thank you to whoever may hear it.

Traffic on this remote highway stretch south of Fredonia wasn't thick at this time in the morning. She would wait until the road was visibly clear behind her to make her move.

A sign said they were entering the Kaibab National Forest area. Another sign said that a sharp turn to the right was coming up and to slow down.

She looked in her mirror. No one was in sight. The corner had small shrubs, which would aid in cover as this area seemed pretty flat and barren.

She gunned the car as hard as she could. In seconds, she was gaining on the trooper quite fast. Little yellow signs with small black arrows told her the road turned to the right. She swung out and smashed the accelerator to the floor again, passing the cruiser doing ninety. To handle the turn, she had to drop her speed hard. With a gentle hand, she pulled back into her lane and hit the brakes as she maneuvered through the beginning of the turn, waiting for the right second to make her move.

The police siren came on behind her.

He was taking her bait. All she needed now was the right spot.

Halfway through the turn, she saw the perfect spot. The shoulder led into a grassy area a foot lower than the road. About ten feet from the shoulder were small trees and shrubs.

Sarah jerked the car off Highway 89 and hit the grass. She had slowed it down to fifty miles an hour by this time. She aimed for the shrubs, careful to drive the Nissan deep enough so it wouldn't be spotted from the highway. The trooper wouldn't follow in here with his car, giving her time to prepare.

The Nissan slid to a stop before a rock formation, bumping it softly. She killed the engine and turned around. All she saw was green. She could not see the highway anymore.

With her gun in hand, Sarah lowered the window and hopped out of the car. It took her three steps to be completely covered by foliage. Then she waited.

The wait wasn't long. The siren turned off but not the cruiser's engine. Without a car passing on the highway, it was so quiet out here that she even heard his dispatcher talking through his cruiser's open door or window. There was no line of sight, but he would come and have a look. The only question she had now was how long before backup arrived.

Seconds ticked by. The waiting became nerve-wracking.

Then, from the corner of her eye, she saw the trooper approaching. He moved slowly, cautiously, like he was walking into a trap.

What could've led him to think that?

The ground was too soft to hear his footsteps. He was three feet away. Two feet.

Sarah stepped from cover as he passed her.

"Don't," she said as he dropped his hand to the butt of his weapon and crouched in a spin. "Just don't. Easy now, raise those hands."

He did as instructed. The holster un-clicked without

trouble, and Sarah lifted his gun out while placing her own against the side of his neck.

"Easy, take it easy, and you will walk away from this."

"You may not, missus. I'm a state trooper. You're in a lot of trouble now."

"If you only knew," she said as she shoved his gun into the back of her pants. She stepped around to face him. "Take off your jacket, slowly. No hero stuff. I'm jittery, and this gun could go off by accident. Any sudden moves, you're dead, and I'm long gone."

The cop removed his jacket with caution. Small beads of sweat formed on his forehead. "You're that girl from the truck stop. Something has happened to you. Maybe I can help instead of you running scared like this."

"You are helping. Toss the jacket away and remove your handcuffs. Then put them on your wrists in the front."

He threw his jacket aside and paused. "Are you sure about this? Do you know how much trouble you're in right now? I can help. Put the gun down, and I will tell them you had an accident because you were nervous when you saw the cruiser, and you didn't want to tell on whomever it was that hurt you. Let me in, and I can help."

"As I said, you are helping, but you cease to be of service if you keep talking because you're delaying me. Now, the cuffs."

He crossed his arms and shook his head in the negative. "I won't cuff myself. You're going to have to do it."

Sarah dropped her weapon a few inches and fired. The report was deafening in the early morning silence. The response from the young officer was what she wanted. He crouched down with both hands raised and shouted compliance.

"Okay, okay, don't shoot. Don't shoot. I'll do it. I'll do it."

The bullet hit a rock just behind his right foot, ricocheting off into the trees. The ricochet sound was just as scary as the gunfire because she had no idea where the bullet would end up.

The trooper cuffed himself and stood back up to his full height of six feet. On any other day, Sarah would have assessed how *hot* he was, but today she had to be all business.

"Now what?" he asked.

Sarah reached into her pocket and pulled out the Nissan's key fob. Holding down the trunk button popped the lid. She eased over, never taking her eyes off the trooper, and lifted the trunk.

"Get in."

"Are you serious? It's going to get very hot later today. I could die."

"I will tell someone you're here, but not until after lunch. In the meantime, I parked it among these little trees. The car will be in the shade until at least three or four this afternoon. Now get in, or I will shoot you in the leg and drag you in. Bleeding to death will be your primary concern then."

A large vehicle passed on the highway going slowly through the long curve in the road. The officer halted to see if Sarah would look toward the road.

"Nothing distracts me when I'm on the job," she said. "Get in, now!"

To the trooper's credit, or maybe it was something in Sarah's face that frightened him, he jumped into the trunk like it was a bowl of jelly.

"Scrunch down."

He lowered his head, and Sarah brought the gun up. She pulled the trigger until the last two bullets in her weapon spat out, creating holes in the lid of the trunk.

She tossed the empty gun into the trunk with the cop and pulled his revolver out of the back of her pants.

"What did you do that for?"

"I know what it's like being in a trunk for a long period of time, so I decided to give you breathing holes for when it gets a bit nasty."

Before shutting the lid, she snatched the pepper spray off his belt loop.

"Thanks. I think I'll need this, too."

Sarah shut the lid and tossed the car keys into the bush. She picked his jacket up off the ground, put it on, and ran out to the waiting cruiser.

The engine was still running as she originally heard, the dispatcher still talking. Another truck came up from behind, slowing to take the corner. Sarah ducked down and waited until it passed.

When it was gone, she got in, put the cruiser in drive, turned on the lights and siren, and did a U-turn on Highway 89, heading back toward Fredonia. Just as Gert had taught her four years ago, stealing a police car got you where you wanted to go and fast—but it also added to the risk factor.

A little more preparation, and she'd be ready.

When ready, she would enter the FLDS compound on Six Mile Road and announce that she had arrived.

Chapter 45

A HOCKEY PUCK AT the bottom of a lake would be easier to find than locating Sarah Roberts.

Parkman was still an hour out of Fredonia, and he was lost. Once he got to Fredonia, then what? He had no idea where she was going or what she was attempting to do. Without the proper resources to back him up, it would be difficult to bump into her coincidentally.

All he had was a handwritten note to go on.

He grabbed his cell phone, which still had a decent charge as he hadn't been using it, and called his own department. When the main desk answered, he asked to be put through to Winnfield.

"Yup," Winnfield answered.

"It's Parkman. I need your help."

"My help?" Winnfield yawned. "Why do you need my help? You're still working with the FBI, aren't you?"

"Was I ever working with them?"

"True. What can I do for you?"

"Listen, I'm going to be driving into a town called Fredonia in the next forty-five minutes or so. It's in northern Arizona—"

"What are you doing way down there?"

"Never mind that right now. I can fill you in when I get back. I need you to find out what police calls they've had in the last three to four hours. I'm looking for something strange, not your usual domestic calls. I'm trying to find Sarah Roberts. Can you do that?"

"Yeah, but I might have to go upstairs for this."

"Don't. I need you to do this without anyone knowing. Make up some bogus reason and get the list of calls. There shouldn't be too many as it's only just after seven in the morning. Winnfield, I'm counting on you. Tell me you got this."

"I'll do it, but you owe me."

"Done. I owe you. Call my cell as soon as you have something."

Parkman tossed his cell on the passenger seat, drove on, and waited. It took twenty minutes to hear back. In that time, he had ground through two toothpicks. He popped a third in his mouth and answered the phone.

"Parkman, Winnfield here."

"I know. What do you have?"

"Before I tell you, you should know the dispatcher gave me the run around when I called. I had to tell her you were down there working for the FBI. I dropped Hanover's name. Then the woman hung up on me. I called back, and she answered the phone on the third try, saying she had to verify my story."

"Shit. Does that mean Hanover knows where I am?"

"You didn't tell me she wasn't supposed to know."

"Did you get anything?" Parkman asked as he heard a beep indicating someone was calling through.

"There were two calls around Fredonia itself. Nothing stood out. A rig had blown a tire about two miles north of the city, and some of the rubber had flown into the side of some guy's pickup truck. The other call was about a couple of kids who were found behind some bar sleeping off too much booze. That was it."

Parkman chewed his pick.

"Damn." He smacked the steering wheel.

"You gonna tell me what's going on?"

"It's a long story, and one most people wouldn't believe."

He glanced at the papers beside him, no doubt written by Vivian, a dead girl. "Are you sure there was nothing else?"

"There was a call from a state trooper pulling a car over about forty to fifty miles south of Fredonia, but I didn't think that mattered. Besides, it was something about a car losing control, and an officer was going to offer aid. He hadn't checked back in yet, but that's not unusual, and it's forty or more miles away from Fredonia."

That had to be it. Even if it wasn't, he had nothing else to go on. In his gut, something was telling him to play that one out.

"Anything else on this trooper?"

"Let me look at what I wrote down," Winnfield paused. Parkman heard him tapping a pen. "Lone female driver. Saw her at the truck stop near Fredonia. Bruised face. Passed the cop going eighty, at least. Lost control on the big curve on Highway 89 as she entered the Kaibab National Forest area. That's all the dispatcher had."

"Winnfield, what part of *locate Sarah Roberts* didn't resonate with you? Lone female driver? Bruised face?"

"Yeah, I guess that matches, but you said—"

"Forget it. I'd prefer it if you didn't tell anyone about this. Dump the information you have. I'm going to call Hanover now and let her know. I'll see you when this is over."

He pulled the phone away from his ear and clicked it off as Winnfield asked another question.

Fredonia was at least fifteen minutes away. He had forty more miles to go on the south side. He hit the gas and turned on the dash light. He decided to wait to call Hanover. After he checked this lead, he would call her and explain why he wasn't in contact for the last few hours.

Vivian's message was a wild hunch he would deal with alone. If it panned out, the FBI could swoop down on this barren land within an hour.

He would apologize to Hanover and solve the case.

Or he would apologize and lose his job.

Or worse, he would be brought up on obstruction charges.

Chapter 46

SARAH REACHED SIX MILE Road and turned onto it. She drove slowly to avoid road dust, which would announce her arrival long before she wanted them to know she was in the area.

A rudimentary plan had formed in her mind. Precision was all she needed to execute it.

Within ten miles, she passed a driveway with a locked iron gate. A long driveway heading at least half a mile in was on the other side of the gate. Without slowing the vehicle, Sarah continued down Six Mile Road for another minute until she found an old landfill company that had closed long ago. The building at the back of the lot had boarded-up windows. A chain-link fence surrounded the parking area with a sign that told everyone to keep out.

She pulled into the recess by the gate and stopped. She remembered reading about the fundamentalist Mormons back in early 2008. The FBI invaded a compound in Texas. It stuck with her because they had removed over four hundred children from families with one husband and many wives.

Maybe that was why this compound was such a good cover for people kidnapping young girls. It allowed them to manage their prisoners without the scrutiny of outsiders. One distinctive feature of the Texas compound was the security tower. She'd seen it on an episode of Oprah. They maintained a two-story tower that oversaw the compound. It resembled a small air traffic control tower.

Beside her, on the passenger seat, was the cop's iPhone. He'd left it plugged into the car charger when he got out to investigate her accident. Accessing the record feature, she pressed the button, allowed it to record nothing for three minutes, and then said her message.

After that, she gathered everything she would need, placed the iPhone on the front seat beside her, and turned the cruiser around to start heading back toward the compound.

When she was about thirty feet from the iron-gated entrance, she dropped the gas pedal down and aimed for the center of it. The black bars on the grill of the cruiser smacked the gate hard enough to break it open. A small swerve left and then right was all she encountered as she got the car under control and sped down the long driveway.

She assumed their defenses would be low due to the early hour of her unannounced visit. Hopefully, they weren't so unwelcoming that they'd open fire on a police car.

The guard shack came into view. There was nowhere to turn off the driveway coming into the compound. She would have to continue forward, aimed directly at the shack.

A large white building came into view off to her right. It had to be their temple. Smaller buildings were scattered around the area. As she got within fifty feet of the guard shack, she could see the structures were more like little schoolhouses.

The cruiser caught the attention of two women hurrying along in long blue dresses, their hair in buns. It also caught the attention of the man stepping out of the guard shack.

Sarah grabbed the state trooper's hat, placed it on her head, and ducked down as low as she could in the driver's seat. The last thing she wanted was for this guard to try and stop the vehicle. On this gravel driveway, she'd have difficulty avoiding him at the speed she was going.

Luckily, as she raced by him, he didn't step out to persuade her to stop. All he did was wave his arms to get her attention.

In the rearview mirror, Sarah watched him run back into his shack, probably intent on calling someone.

She drove down the line of blue houses, watching for any sign of resistance. For the size of this compound, she was surprised that she didn't see more people.

At the end of the row of houses, she turned the vehicle away and aimed it down another road that appeared to lead to a fence line. It took mere seconds for Sarah to exit the cruiser, set everything she needed into the trooper's hat, put the car in drive, and shut the door.

The cruiser moved away from her slowly. It went straight for at least twenty feet, then started to angle off the road. Sarah gathered her belongings in the hat and ran to the nearest house.

At this early hour, she assumed everyone would be either still sleeping or performing some task as required by the fundamentalist faith.

Just before reaching the edge of the building and cover, Sarah looked down the stretch of road and saw no one in pursuit. Other than the guard and the two women she saw walking near the front moments ago, the place looked deserted.

As she ran in the open door of the first building, she wondered if Vivian's warning was about to come true. Was this a trap, or did she actually have the wrong location?

The people of this dwelling lived a quiet existence with a couple of chairs and beds lining one wall. Open doors at the back led to another room. Sarah ran for that room, pulling the cop's gun out in case she needed it.

This room was also empty but contained what she was looking for. The closet was full of blue dresses, and the bathroom on the side would allow her to fix her hair right.

In a frantic rush, Sarah found a dress that would fit her, threw it on, and ran for the bathroom. One peek out the window told her no one was outside yet. It wouldn't be long. The guard had to be rallying help.

Using pins, she got her hair tied up in a ball resembling the women she had seen earlier and covered the back of her neck. She found enough pins to securely tie the pepper spray into her hair, hiding it from view.

She looked at herself in the mirror and nodded. It wouldn't pass scrutiny, but it would get her where she needed to go.

Now she was ready except for something to conceal the gun.

Out in the main room, she found a wicker basket. She dropped the gun in the bottom and covered it with a shawl.

Before leaving the building, she took a sidelong look out the window. The guard from the shack was walking up the road accompanied by two other men. They were coming fast.

Sarah waited until they passed the building she was in and watched all three of them start down the road toward the fence where the cruiser had stopped.

She gently opened the window in front of her. Then she ran to every other window and opened them, too. At the front once again, Sarah could see the three men standing by the cruiser, the rest of the street empty.

She set the cop's bullhorn on a little table by the front window and placed the iPhone behind it. With one last look outside, she accessed the iPhone's voice recorder and pressed play on the file she'd recorded earlier in the cruiser.

That gave her three minutes of silence for her run for the temple.

Basket in hand, wearing a long blue dress and her hair in a bun, Sarah left the building and walked as fast as she dared up the road toward the temple. She got to the end of the line of little houses before encountering her first person. They passed each other with the barest of nods. She also passed the test. They thought she was one of them. It made sense to her. Young, pretty, innocent looking, and in their own garb, wouldn't raise too many eyebrows, although the bruised face might.

The three minutes were up as her own voice boomed from the end house. It traveled through the crisp morning air causing goosebumps on her arms.

"We have you surrounded. This is the FBI."

Even now, she doubted its veracity. Listening to it from afar only made her sound ridiculous.

As she neared the temple, she decided to try a back or side entrance. A turn to the left took her down a narrow road toward the back.

People were streaming out the back of the temple. Dozens and dozens of women were running for the road, heading for a smaller building that resembled an office complex.

Sarah turned away and walked up and into the nearest house, her basket swinging in her arms.

Again, this residence was empty. Evidently, the advantage of living in a gated compound was leaving all the doors unlocked.

She wondered why she was being so cautious. Normally she would've walked right up and joined the fleeing women to wherever they were headed. She was dressed just like them, and she'd already passed one without batting an eye. Could it be that Vivian's warning scared her into being too cautious? Every minute counted. Why waste time hiding? By now, they would've discovered the recording was a fake, so that ruse was wasted. Maybe that's why they were taking the members and hustling them to a hiding spot.

She walked to the front door and stepped out onto the porch. That was when one of Armond's men, gun in hand, ran down the road toward her. He stood out with his black leather jacket.

She hesitated, looked in her basket, and turned back around to walk into the house. Once inside, she pulled the gun out and flipped off the safety. In a crouch, Sarah bent below the front window, peering out to watch where Armond's man went.

He stopped in front of the house.

"Hello in there?" he shouted.

Should I respond or not?

"I saw you go in. Hello?"

"Yes," Sarah hollered back.

"We're gathering everyone in the basement opposite the temple. We think the police are attempting some kind of inspection, so leave this building at once and get to the basement."

"Okay. I'll be along in a minute."

She peeked back out. Armond's man turned and headed away from her, running down the road toward where she ditched the cop car.

With her gun back in the basket and the shawl neatly placed, Sarah left the building and started up the road toward the temple. The women were still coming out of the temple, now followed by dozens of small children.

When she got close, she saw another of Armond's men standing at the entrance. She would've seen him earlier if it hadn't been for the sun in her eyes. With no real plan other than to surprise them, she was running out of options. These people were hired killers, and she was trying to liberate their captives. As much as she wanted to do this on her own, she was starting to feel underprepared and overwhelmed.

The guy at the door watched every face as they entered the building, so he hadn't seen her falter yet. She turned away from him and headed for the temple. A couple of the women said things like, "No, this way," and "to the basement," but Sarah only nodded and kept moving to the temple.

Without looking, she almost bumped into the back of the third man in a black leather jacket.

She made to walk past him as the last few people left the building, but the guy grabbed her arm.

"No, it's the other way. We need everyone to get to the —" He stopped suddenly, probably recognizing her and the bruise he put on her face.

Not one second later, a bullet from Sarah's gun hit him in the center of his throat.

His grip tightened on her arm in a spasm, and then he let go. He went for his weapon but covered his wound, blood seeping through his fingers in gushing spurts. Slowly, he slipped down the wall, eyes wide.

For a moment, Sarah lost touch with what was happening around her. A couple of women ran up and stared wide-eyed at the man bleeding on the floor.

"Get a doctor," Sarah said. "This man needs help."

She followed them to the door and shut it behind them. She set her basket down and pulled two chairs over to keep the doors shut.

When she picked up her basket and turned around, another FLDS woman stood staring at her.

"We're a quiet people," the woman said. "What have you done? Why would you do this in our temple? This is the worst crime." The woman's eyes watered.

"Wrong, sister. In your sheltered compound life, you have no idea what real assholes like this one are doing. They have been kidnapping young girls and using them as sex slaves, and they're hiding them here, in your compound. I have come to take them home."

"You want to remove our children? Is that what you want?"

"No, not your children—"

The woman cut her off. "We are a peaceful people," she said, shaking her head.

"Yeah, well, so am I. You may be able to avoid the real world in your compound, but when they bring their victims here, then it becomes my problem."

A high-pitched squeal came from somewhere above.

"I thought everyone was evacuated," Sarah said.

"Everyone was." A stunned look crossed the woman's face.

"Then what's upstairs?" Sarah asked.

"Rooms."

"Rooms for what?"

"It's where the babies are baptized, and sometimes new wives consummate their marriages."

"You serious? In the temple?"

The woman looked at her. "Am I serious about what?"

"Nothing. If you want to live, you might want to get across the road to the basement like everyone else."

Sarah dropped the basket and held the cop's gun firmly in her right hand. With one man down, they would know she was here or think the authorities were closing in.

The woman moved toward the door. She didn't look back at Sarah. The door swung open easily after the chair was pushed aside, and then she was gone.

Alone in this large, cavernous temple, Sarah started for the side, walking by the pews. She found the stairs and started up them as quietly as she could. There were no more sounds from upstairs except for the usual scuffling of people moving around.

It took her almost no time at all to get to the top of the stairs. A small hallway led to three closed doors. She paused and looked back down into the temple below, allowing herself to catch her breath. If it weren't for the constant scuffling sounds of people moving around on this level, it would feel like the whole building was empty.

With the silence of a ballet dancer, Sarah stayed close to the wall and moved beside the first door to listen. After hearing nothing, she moved to the next door. A soft thump and another scuffle told her the movement was coming from behind door number three.

She hadn't been trained on how to enter a room. All she knew how to do was surprise them with speed and be violent to get their attention fast.

She knocked the door open with one hard shoulder bump and a quick twist of the door handle. It flew around so hard that it hit the other wall with a bang.

Sarah, the gun in front, jumped into the room. As soon as she crossed the threshold, a wooden club dropped down onto her right wrist, snapping it with a loud audible crack. The gun flew from her grip, along with the hope of getting out of there alive.

She couldn't believe the pain. Her wrist was instantly on fire. From the moment the wood broke her wrist to the moment she found herself on her knees leaning into the doorframe, she hadn't even seen who was in the room yet.

Water glazed over her eyes. She had to blink it away to see the five teenage girls staring back at her. Forlorn eyes, saddened by the knowledge that death wasn't far away, deepened by a depression that had stolen their innocence, the girls stared back at the person who had come for them, the one person who might have helped them leave this nightmare behind. What stared back at them was a beat-up girl just past her own teenage horror, now wounded to immobility.

Sarah held her wrist, moaning and rocking back and forth as swelling set in.

Jack Tate, or Armond Stuart, as she had come to know

him, stepped out from behind the door, grinning.

"Glad you could join us. I finally get to kill you, you meddling bitch."

Chapter 47

THE NISSAN HADN'T BEEN hard to find. The land out this way was vast and barren. On this particular curve in the road, Parkman could easily see the tire treads of a recent skid mark where a vehicle left the road. He pulled over and got out. The sun was higher now, the heat rising with it. By the time he got off the shoulder and walked toward the shrubbery, his shirt had pasted to his back.

The rear of the Nissan came into view. He pulled his piece out and approached with caution. A vehicle raced by on the highway. Then something moved near the car. Or was it the car that moved?

"Hello? Anybody there?"

The voice came from the car. There were two bullet holes in the trunk lid. A quick sweep of the area confirmed no one was waiting to ambush him.

"This is the police. Identify yourself," Parkman said.

"Oh, hey, get me outta here. I'm Andre Wilson, an Arizona state trooper. Some girl got the jump on me. She tricked me and stuffed me in the trunk."

Sarah Roberts, that's my girl ...

"Did this girl have a bruise on her cheek?"

"Yes, yes. Now get me out of here."

Parkman holstered his weapon. "Okay, hold on. If the car is unlocked, I'll pop the trunk."

He walked around and opened the driver's side door. Beside the driver's seat, he flipped the trunk button. Scattered papers lie askew on the passenger seat. Parkman picked them up and pocketed them as he got out of the car.

He walked around to the back and saw the trooper crawling out, his hands cuffed in the front.

"You doing okay?" Parkman asked. "How long were you in there?"

The trooper got to the ground and stood. "I don't know, probably an hour and a half, maybe two hours. Hard to tell. I have to admit, there were times when I wondered if someone would find me, but I kept reassuring myself that I'd called the stop-in, so it would only be a matter of time. Where are you from?"

Parkman had grabbed his cuff keys and began working on releasing the trooper's wrists. "Long way from here. I've been trailing that girl for hundreds of miles. Did she say anything about where she was going?"

Andre shook his head. "No, nothing. She followed me until these trees could give her coverage and then made me come in after her when she ran off the highway. I should have seen it coming. She's good, but it pissed me off that I could be duped so easily."

Parkman nodded. The cuffs flipped open. "If you only knew how good this girl is. And trust me, she pisses a lot of people off. Let me call this in and get one of your colleagues to pick you up."

Andre was already walking away from him, but he was heading toward the trees, away from the highway. "Go ahead, call it in. I gotta take a piss. I was holding it to see if I got out in time. Didn't want to soil my uniform."

Parkman turned around, pulled out his cell phone, and dialed Hanover while reading the papers he took from the front seat of the Nissan. By the time Hanover answered, he had recognized the notes for what they were and knew what needed to be done.

"Jill Hanover here."

"Hanover, it's Parkman."

"Where the hell are you?"

"Fredonia, Arizona. I'm tracking Sarah Roberts."

"Fredonia? Why is she in Fredonia?"

"Look, how fast can you get down here?"

"Why?" Hanover asked.

"Something big is going down at an address on Six Mile Road. I don't know what yet, but I can tell you we need to be there."

Andre walked up beside him. "What's this I hear about Six Mile Road?"

"Hanover, hold on a sec." Parkman lowered the phone. He lifted the paper with the address on it. "Do you know what is located at this address?"

"Sure, it's a huge fundamentalist Mormon compound. A gated and secured facility."

Parkman lifted a finger to get Andre to wait.

"Hanover, I think Sarah's in trouble. She stole a police car, and I can assure you she has singlehandedly broken into a gated Mormon compound."

"Stole a police car? Broke into a compound? Why would she do that?"

"Probably because that's where the perps have taken their captives. It sounds like a perfect hiding place." He motioned for Andre to follow and started for the car. "It's how she operates. But this time, I'm afraid she may be in over her head. How long before you can get here?"

"I'm on my way. I have a chopper. It shouldn't be more than an hour."

Parkman pocketed his cell and jumped in his car. Andre got in the other side.

"Direct me to this compound," Parkman said. "We need to get there quick."

He performed a U-turn, hit the lights, and dropped the accelerator.

"We can't just walk in," Andre said. "That's one of the heaviest guarded compounds in the area. Remember what happened in Texas back in 2008?"

"I have a feeling the front gate will be wide open."

Chapter 48

"GET OVER THERE WITH the others where I can see you," Armond said.

Sarah got up and stumbled to the wall to sit with the other girls. The raw edge of the pain had abated, becoming a dull ache, throbbing with her pulse. She cleared her eyes and dropped back down to the floor. She had to stay focused. There was no way she could let it end here.

"I have waited years for this," Armond said. "We had it planned so well. Did you know that?"

Sarah shook her head in the negative. Armond had already picked up her weapon and put it in his waistband. He'd closed the door and called someone on his cell phone, telling them to let him know when they had the all-clear. Sarah knew the all-clear would come shortly, and when Armond's associates showed up, it would all be over.

"The girl's body by my house was to throw the Feds off," Armond said. "They've been tracking me for too long. I can't lead a private life anymore. If they thought someone else did that killing, maybe they would leave me alone because I knew they were trying to pin her kidnapping on me. My boys are creatures of habit, so they ripped her shirt like they were supposed to. But fuck if they didn't screw up."

He walked to the door and placed an ear against it. Then he turned back to her. "Ever since you killed Alex, my brother, by the way, and not my son, I have wanted to kill you in the most severe ways. But you moved out of your parents' home and stayed on the move. I have a business to run," he paused and swung his arm in an arc, indicating the girls sitting alongside her, "so I couldn't spend all my time trying to deal with you."

One of the girls beside Sarah was crying. It was a subtle sobbing that didn't elicit a response from Armond. Whatever motivation Sarah had to kill Armond shot up tenfold.

"It was all planned," he said again as he paced in front of her. "I was supposed to go your parents' house, get them to invite you over, and I'd murder them in front of you when you got there. That would be payback for my brother. Nice, huh?"

He stared at her, his eyes filled with hatred.

"Then, I would take my time killing you. But you fucked all that up. If you hadn't shown up like you did and shot my man and then dropped the other one, you and your parents would be dead right now. How did you know to be there at that precise moment? And what made you think they were going to kill me?"

The realization of what had happened hit Sarah hard. Her sister had saved her life. By sending her into this mess, Sarah had avoided being killed. That meant Vivian wasn't fighting her and sending her into risky situations. Instead, she was trying her best to keep Sarah alive.

"It doesn't matter now," Armond continued. "You walked straight into my hands. This is a secured compound. The regular authorities don't come around here, and the leader of this place does what I tell him to. If he doesn't, he loses out on a lot of money. Without that, he's done."

"Why involve my parents?" Sarah asked.

"We were supposed to kill them. Keeping them alive was only to get to you. Then you escaped somehow, so I had to trade them for Sam, hoping he could tell me what the police knew about you, as you were always my priority."

"It's not over yet. I will kill you before this is done," Sarah said.

Armond stepped back. "What did you say? Could you repeat it?"

"I said, I will kill you before this is done. You have my word on that," Sarah said. Even through the pain, she remained rooted, eyes unwavering, hatred unchecked.

"My, what big aspirations for a beat-up little girl with a broken wrist and no *fucking gun*!"

"The police are on their way or already here. You're through, Armond. It's over. Now, give me your gun so I can ensure you never see the inside of a prison cell. You don't look like the type to be someone's bitch. You know what they do to cops on the inside?"

Armond laughed. "You are some piece of work. Even with the odds stacked against you, you're still feisty. What's stopping me from pointing this weapon and pulling the trigger right here, right now?"

"Nothing, except you know that if I'm telling the truth, you could use me to bargain a deal. Then, you could take another shot at me once this blows over."

"No," Armond waved the weapon in the air. "I've got these beauties I could bargain with. I *have* to kill you. You murdered my brother."

He lifted his weapon, aiming it at Sarah. The girls around her moved away in a scurrying motion.

Sarah turned away and, using her good hand, balanced herself to her feet and then to a full standing position. When she turned back around, the gun was aimed at her forehead from five feet away.

Armond's cell phone rang. Without missing a beat, he pulled it out and answered it. A moment later, he pocketed the phone and lowered his weapon.

"You have won a five-minute reprieve. I'm being told you were alone when you showed up here, but chatter on the scanner in the security radio room has possible police presence on their way. Don't move. Just stay where you are, or I'll aim for your crotch to see how you take a bullet. Trust me. I'm a sadistic bastard."

When he stopped speaking, Armond backed up to the door. He opened it and stepped into the hallway while keeping an eye on her.

She took a deep breath and leaned into the wall to collect herself. The knowledge that Vivian orchestrated her presence here got her through that moment.

Maybe someone found the Nissan with the cop in the trunk. It's likely the cop she put in the trunk had called in to report the traffic stop/accident. Once he was let out of the trunk, they would find Vivian's note on the seat, leading them here. But would they come to ask around, looking for her? Or would they come armed and ready to attack a compound?

She guessed the former, which meant she still needed to do this on her own.

She turned around to the girls assembled by her. "It's okay. This is almost over. You are all going home soon."

Footsteps pounded up the hall. The guy who told her to leave the house and go to the basement earlier stood in the doorway.

"Okay, girls," he said. "Everyone up. This is all over. I want everyone to leave with Armond except for you, Sarah."

The girls got up and filed out of the room, some visibly crying. The last girl at the door turned and said, "My name is Jennifer. I just wanted you to know that. Thank you."

"How sweet," Armond said and pushed the girl out. "Sarah, my friend here will make you uncomfortable for five minutes until I return to kill you. Please enjoy his company." Armond turned to his man. "Watch yourself with this one. She's a tough bitch."

"She's beat up and has a broken wrist. I didn't survive Desert Storm to be taken out by this piece of shit," the guy said, looking Sarah up and down.

The door shut hard behind Armond as he stepped out, leaving them alone.

"How do you want to do this?" Sarah asked. "You wanna fuck first? Or should I kill you and then fuck your corpse?"

"That's some mouth you have for a pretty girl," he said.

In a quick movement, he stepped close and elbowed her in the face. The blow knocked her back into the wall, where she slid to the floor.

Blackness formed around her eyes. She couldn't pass out. If she passed out, it would be over. A part of her wondered why she struggled.

Let it go. Let it go.

The guy removed his jacket. He pulled his arms out of his shoulder holster next. "I understand your family knows Armond intimately."

Sarah wondered what that meant. In her foggy mind, she couldn't figure out what he was talking about. He was removing his shirt now. Blood seeped out of her mouth, where he hit her. The pain numbed her consciousness.

"Did you know that the crazy fundamentalists consummate their marriages to fourteen and sixteen-year-olds in this room? I understand it was a room just like this where Armond defiled your sister almost twenty years ago. Did you know that it was Armond who raped and murdered Vivian?"

A fire raged inside her. The throbbing pain fueled hatred so deep that no pain could subdue it. Sarah reached up to the back of her neck and pulled a small clump of hair out.

"Hey, what're you doing? That's fucking gross, man. Isn't that painful?" He stopped undressing to watch her.

Her scalp ached as it did years ago when she pulled. Sarah felt power and strength like never before. She grabbed another patch and ripped it out. The pain felt sweet and delicious. She remembered a time when this pain was a comfort when she needed it to get through the day. That was a long time ago. She'd healed since then, but right now, the exhilarating rush became addictive. On her third pull, she saw the guy's face distort.

"You are seriously *fucked*," he said.

She leaned hard against the wall and pushed herself up. "I love this," she said. "Pulling my hair out takes me back to another time when I killed people like you. You don't get a judge. You don't get a jury. You get *me*."

"You're actually nuts, aren't you? You're fucking crazy."

He moved toward her. She reached back again, her head clear now, the dark buzzing around her vision gone. Under the pins that she'd placed carefully in her hair, she found the pepper spray bottle. With her thumb, she unclasped the safety. He was right in front of her now, his arm pulling back to hit her.

Sarah tore at the bottle, ripped it out, and sprayed it from two feet away directly into his eyes and mouth while she screamed as if she was an escapee from the rubber room.

He staggered away from her, clutching at his eyes, his breathing coming in ragged pants. After her scream, Sarah closed her eyes to slits and held her breath. She was still too close to risk breathing. She ducked down, grabbed his gun from the holster on the floor, and aimed it at his crotch. Then she flipped the safety and fired.

Blood shot out where his penis should be. He dropped to the floor, screaming like a man should never scream.

Sarah made a beeline for the door, but before she got there, Armond opened it.

He had a gun out and pointed at her from seven feet away.

His weapon spat loud and clear.

She didn't get a chance to shoot as Armond's bullet caught her on the left side of her chest, knocking her off balance and spinning her down to the floor.

As she lost consciousness, an odd thought struck her.

Where did all the blood on Armond's face come from?

Chapter 49

SARAH ROLLED HER EYES, trying to open them. The pain kept her from moving. Her head ached. Everything felt tired, sore, and pissed off.

She tried again. Dim light entered her eyelids. A hospital room. Flowers to her right, flowers to her left. Dull hospital paint on the wall.

She moved her head slowly to see if she was alone. A pain shot up from somewhere in her chest.

A man sat in a chair, reading a book. He looked like a cop.

His head rose. Her eyes shut.

Too much pain. She passed out.

***

There was noise in the room. People milled about. A man talked.

"She woke and looked at me ... then closed her eyes

again."

"How long ago did this happen?" Her mother's voice.

"About an hour."

"Okay, everyone," a different man said. "I'm sure she'll wake up again soon. Let's try to keep our voices down and our hopes up. Amelia, your daughter is strong. She's a fighter. I'm confident she'll pull through. The operation was a success. Now we wait."

"I know, I know, I just …"

Sarah slept.

***

Movement around her again.

She opened her eyes. Too bright. The sun shone through the window across her body, warming her under the covers. The pain had subsided to something bearable.

A nurse stood close. They looked at each other. Then, with the professionalism expected of her, the nurse calmly walked around the bed, lifted a glass of water, and applied the bendable straw to Sarah's lips. Her throat felt ragged. The water cut at first, then soothed.

She tried to speak when the straw pulled out but failed as her throat's fire wasn't diminished yet.

"Rest," the nurse said. "Relax. I'll get the doctor. Your mother has been with you since you got here. She's in the cafeteria. I'll let her know you're awake."

"How …" she tried. Then again. "How … long?"

"How long have you been here?" The nurse asked for clarification.

Sarah nodded slowly.

"Almost a month. I'll get the doctor. He'll explain everything."

Minutes later, her mother entered the room.

"Sarah, you're awake. Oh, baby, it's so good to have you back."

Her mother hugged her arm, no doubt afraid to touch her anywhere else. She sobbed, tears running along Sarah's forearm.

"Don't cry, Mom."

She let go and wiped her eyes. "Tell me, Sarah. Talk to me. What happened this time? Why did it all go wrong? You help people all the time, but nothing like this happens. Why didn't Vivian help?"

"Vivian did. She … saved us … all. Without … her, we would … be dead."

"I don't understand," Amelia said, raising a hand to her mouth.

She's getting more emotional as she ages.

"I will … explain everything when I come home."

A man in a white lab coat entered the room.

"Glad to see you're awake. My name is Doctor Rosenberg. How are you feeling?"

"Not good. I hate being shot."

"You have a sense of humor. Good, I like that. It's a good sign."

"Can I go home now?"

"Not yet. More bed rest for you, young lady. You've been through a lot. I don't get many patients as strong as you, though." The doctor reached for a clipboard at the end of the bed.

"I go home or walk out of here," Sarah said. "I'll let you

… decide."

The doctor smiled. "They told me you were feisty, but you won't be able to walk out of here for at least a week. You've been shot numerous times. Lucky for you, two of the bullet wounds only needed stitches. You were hit so hard in the face that the orbital bone around your eye is bruised. The worst was the bullet that entered your chest just left of your heart. It's a miracle that it missed all bones and any major organs. All it did was lodge itself beside your heart. When you were brought in for surgery, we successfully removed it. For the trauma you've experienced, I'd say you're lucky to be alive."

Sarah nodded. "I'm still … leaving."

The doctor smiled. "Tell me, do you get this strength from your mother or father?"

"My sister."

"Your sister? I'm sorry, I didn't know you had a sister."

"She died … when I was a baby. We still chat … once in a while."

The doctor, unsettled now, stepped back and edged around Sarah's mother.

"I'll leave you two alone to catch up," he said after slipping the clipboard back on the end of the bed. Then he disappeared through the door.

"Sarah, he's been good to you. Why did you do that?"

"I want out of here. I hate … hospitals."

"I know. I'll get your father and see when we can take you home."

Tiredness crept up on her. She didn't want to sleep. She needed to know how it all turned out first. Was she a sitting duck, just waiting for Armond to walk in and kill her? Why else would they have a police guard in her hospital room?

"Tell me how I got … here. What happened?"

"I can help with that," a man said.

Parkman walked into view.

"I had a hell of a time trying to keep on your tail after you ran away from me at the hangar. I found your note in the motel waste basket and your other note in the Nissan where you put the cop in the trunk. Sarah, you might want to try trusting me. One of these days, you could get killed for real."

He stepped closer. Sarah could smell his cologne. Sleep called, causing her eyes to close. She forced them open, determined to sleep in peace with the knowledge that Armond, her sister's killer, was dead.

"Tell me … more."

Parkman grabbed a chair beside the bed, turned it backward, and straddled it. Her mother walked to the door, closed it, and then stood at the foot of the bed.

"When I got to the compound," Parkman started, "the gates were broken, so I drove right in, knowing you might be in trouble. I'd already called the FBI. You might remember Agent Jill Hanover from four years ago. She had an FBI team en route. Within ten minutes of their security giving me the runaround, the FBI showed up, and we recognized Armond. The condensed story is he fired on us, and we fired back."

"Is that … why I saw blood on his face?"

"Yes, it must've been. But Sarah, you're a hero. Did you know that he had a total of eighteen girls? All of them were hospitalized and then released. Two of them were runaways. I also wanted you to know that no formal charges have been filed against you. Andre, the trooper you stuck in the trunk, said he would never have believed you if you told him about the kidnapped girls at the compound. For you to take his car and ram the gates to free them was very brave."

"Where is … Armond Stuart?"

"Everyone was arrested at the compound. Even the fundamentalist leader is being brought up on a host of unrelated charges regarding how young some of his wives are."

Sleep forced her under. She fought back. Sleep could be such an enemy. She would let it in when she was ready.

"Where is … Armond? You're avoiding …"

Parkman looked at her mother. Then he turned and looked down at his shoes. "We don't know."

She moved her left shoulder on purpose. The pain was sharp, but it woke her enough to glare at him.

"What?" she asked, her teeth clenched, her head raised off the pillow.

Parkman returned her stare. "When we got upstairs, he'd disappeared. You were bleeding heavily from your chest wound. The FBI helicopter was still outside. Andre and I picked you up, raced downstairs, and ordered the chopper to bring you here. When we re-joined the search, I was informed that he had somehow escaped. In the cavernous rooms on the temple's top floor, there are hidden areas with crawl spaces behind the wall panels. We didn't know about them until it was too late."

Sarah dropped her head back to the pillow. "So that's … why I have … a cop in my room."

Parkman said something. Her eyes shut.

The pain in her shoulder ebbed.

Sleep was merciful. Sleep was a friend now. She welcomed it. If only to turn the world off for a little while.

Sarah dozed, not waking again for fifteen hours.

***

It was a warm sunny day in late August when her father wheeled her out of the hospital and into his car, to the doctor's chagrin.

Now a month later, in her old bedroom, her mother doting over her every wish, Sarah wrote furiously.

Vivian gave her instructions. Together they plotted. The odds weren't great, but she was prepared to take her chances.

This time, she decided not to be so nice. What's there to lose? She should be dead right now. Vivian said when Sarah dies, they will be reunited. But it's not something Sarah should be focusing on.

She called her father into her room to set the plan into motion.

Within forty-eight hours, she would be on Armond's tail again. Human garbage shouldn't be allowed to breathe the same air as the rest of the population, especially the young girls they prey on.

Next time, when they met again, she was going to make sure the first thing she did was shoot him twice.

Once for Vivian and once for her.

As close as they could be, Sarah and Vivian were hunting on earth and in heaven.

And Armond Stuart was her prey.

Chapter 50

ONE MONTH LATER …

Parkman knocked on their door a second time. He stepped back into the sun, letting its heat soak through his light satin shirt. Today was his second attempt at quitting the toothpicks. It was unsanitary, unattractive, and uncool. Every once in a while, he caught himself moving his tongue around, trying to flip the pick to the other side of his lips, but nothing was there.

He knocked for the third time.

Footsteps approached. The curtain on the side window pulled back, and Caleb's face peered out. The deadbolt was unlatched, and the door swung open.

"Parkman," Caleb greeted him.

"I came by to see how Sarah's doing. It's my day off, and I wanted to talk to her."

"Come on in."

Caleb stepped aside to allow him entrance. The foyer was

wide, with ample room for both men to stand a few feet apart. Caleb didn't move for the stairs or call up to Sarah. He just stared at Parkman.

"Can you get her for me?" Parkman asked. "Or should I just go up to her room?"

Caleb gestured for the living room behind Parkman. "Please, come in, sit down and let me get you a drink. What'll you have?"

"Nothing, I'm fine."

They moved into the living room. The couch faced the smaller loveseat. He sat on the loveseat and waited for Caleb to sit, too.

"What's going on, Caleb?" Parkman asked.

Caleb reached into his pocket and pulled out a folded piece of paper. "This will explain everything."

"What do you mean *everything*? Where's Sarah?"

"She's gone."

"Gone?" Parkman asked, stunned. "Gone where?"

Caleb shrugged.

"Caleb, what are you saying? Her wrist just had the cast removed. She's not physically ready to be *going* anywhere. Armond is still out there."

"I know. That's who she's after."

"What? Have you all gone crazy? That guy is a psychopath. He's a master at this. Sarah can't do it alone." Parkman ran a hand through his hair. He shook his head, trying to get the information that just entered it to jumble around and make sense.

"What have the police ever done for Sarah?" Caleb asked. "You tell me?"

"If it weren't for me, Sarah would be dead. I shot

Armond."

"She told me what happened. I respect that you were on his tail, but seriously, Sarah has always dealt her own cards. Sarah and Vivian can handle this." Caleb smirked. "I have faith in my girls."

"Caleb. Seriously. You need to let me in on this. The FBI didn't press any charges, but I can tell you if Sarah gets out there and people start dying again, they may incarcerate her, not just to keep her safe, but to keep others safe from her."

Caleb leaned forward and clasped his hands together on his legs. "Are you threatening Sarah or me?"

"Come on, Caleb. You know I'm not. But you're her father. You can't sign off on this."

"Already did. She's gone to ground. No one will find her. Consider her disappeared."

Parkman looked away so Caleb wouldn't see his anger and frustration.

"Vivian was taken from us in a shopping mall," Caleb said. "She was raped and murdered. No one found the asshole that did it. It almost tore my family apart. Then Sarah grows up, and she begins acting weird. Four years ago, she starts writing prophecies and helping people survive where, without her, they wouldn't have. Then the same people who killed Vivian take Sarah and almost kill her." He stopped and looked into Parkman's eyes. "Vivian and Sarah have a plan. I've heard parts of it. I like it. So I backed it."

"What do you mean, *backed* it?"

"I withdrew enough money yesterday so Sarah could do what she needs to do to find Armond. She's gone into hiding in case he's looking for her. She has an idea of where he might be in a few days. We know that Armond has already met with a plastic surgeon. He's changed his appearance. That's why you guys will never find him. And he's in Europe, which is a little far from your jurisdiction, anyway."

Parkman blew air out of his mouth.

This is crazy.

"Okay, supposing you're right—" he said.

"I am right."

"Okay, fine. You should know this is going to piss off a lot of people who want to keep close tabs on a girl like Sarah."

"We all know that. That's one of the main reasons she's doing it this way. And what do we care who we piss off? Excuse my language, but fuck that. I had a daughter who was raped and murdered, and the only person doing anything about it is Sarah. And damn it, she almost got the asshole. What are the authorities doing about it? Walking around and asking questions, that's what."

Parkman was stunned. He was sure his face showed it.

"Look, I'm sorry," Caleb said. "That's not fair in light of how you were there at the end of this thing. All I'm trying to say is *you* have to play by the rules. The bad guys don't. Sarah doesn't play by the rules. She's our only chance for justice."

Parkman looked down at the paper in his hand. He unfolded it and read the few words Sarah had written for him.

My friend Parkman,
Don't try to find me. I'm gone.
I will call you when I have something. Keep your phone on.
You are the only cop I trust. Don't let me down when the

day comes when I need you.

If you don't hear from me within six months, consider me dead and gone to live with my sister.

Love, Sarah

P.S. Thanks for being there. I'll always remember you.

"So that's it?" Parkman asked. "I'm just supposed to walk away?"

"Yes," Caleb nodded. "Let it go. Sarah will handle it and contact you if and when she needs to. Sorry, it has to be so brutal, but this is a family matter now."

"Fuck," Parkman slammed a fist into his other palm. He pocketed the crumpled paper and strode to the foyer.

At the door, he turned back around and asked, "Do you have any toothpicks?"

About Jonas Saul

Jonas Saul is the bestselling author of the Sarah Roberts Series—more than two million sold!—and has written and published over sixty thrillers. After acquiring an agent, he signed several deals in Los Angeles, with MadRiver Pictures optioning his Sarah Roberts Series— over forty books!—(currently in development).

Jonas has often outranked Stephen King and Dean

Koontz on Amazon over the past decade. He's regularly invited to be a guest speaker, teacher, or workshop presenter at international writing conferences and film festivals worldwide. He hosts an annual writer's retreat in Greece, where he currently lives. He focuses his teaching on how to get tension and emotion in every scene, on every page, how he made it as a creator/writer, the path to success in this business, and the pitfalls to avoid. He also hosts a reading retreat in Greece with guest authors, yoga retreats, and hiking retreats. Visit the Imagine Greece Retreats website at www.imaginegreeceretreats.com, or email him directly to discuss an opportunity to join one of the retreats at jonas@imaginegreeceretreats.com.

Jonas is also a professional freelance editor. He works for several publishers and does private editing for clients, with many testimonials on his website at www.imaginepress.org, which details each author's response to Jonas's editing skills. Email Jonas directly for an editing quote at editor@imaginepress.org.

To book Jonas for a speaking engagement at a writer's conference/festival, to have him on your jury at a film festival, or even to say hello, email Jonas directly at jonassaul@icloud.com.

For updates on releases, hit the "Follow" button on Amazon or Bookbub, and join Jonas on Facebook, where he's most active.

Contact Jonas Saul

Linktree: Find me here

Email: jonassaul@icloud.com